AT PADDY THE BEAVER'S POND

AT PADDY THE BEAVER'S POND

A Book of Nature Stories by

THORNTON W. BURGESS

Illustrated by

HARRISON CADY

LITTLE, BROWN AND COMPANY

BOSTON · 1950

jB912ap

*Published simultaneously
in Canada by McClelland and Stewart Limited*

PRINTED IN THE UNITED STATES OF AMERICA

Contents

AT PADDY THE BEAVER'S POND

I. The Home Builders

A home is more than just a house,
Be it for Man or Bird or Mouse.
— OLD MOTHER NATURE

DEEP in the Green Forest, at the foot of the Great Mountain, a new home was being built by two busy workers. And how they worked! The time was short before Jack Frost would interfere and there still was much, so very much, to be done. They were Paddy the Beaver and Mrs. Paddy. They had left their old home far down Laughing Brook because not enough food trees remained to supply all the bark they and their children would need through the coming winter. So the old home was left to the young folks.

Now, deep in the Green Forest, they were starting over again as they had done more than once before. There was a dam to build to make a pond. There was a house to build. There was a winter supply of food logs to be cut and stored. And they had only a few weeks in which to do all this before the freeze-up when Jack Frost would put an end to such work until another year.

They didn't know it then but really they were doing more than making a new home for just themselves. That small pond, as yet hardly more than a big puddle, was the beginning of a community center, a meeting place for the furred and feathered folk in all that part of the Green Forest. As yet only King Eagle, who flying high overhead had looked down on the busy workers, and Mrs. Flathorns the Moose, who had chanced to wander that way, knew what was going on. So, undisturbed by prowling enemies, Paddy and Mrs. Paddy worked both night and day. However, they were nonetheless watchful. They knew full well that sooner or later someone with a longing for a Beaver dinner would discover them, and so it proved.

How news travels none shall say, but travel it does and swiftly. It was only a short time before news of that new home had spread all through the Green Forest.

"It is out," declared Paddy one day as he was looking over the small dam.

"What is out?" asked Mrs. Paddy as she worked a stick in where it would do the most good.

"The news that we are here," replied Paddy. He was looking down at something. Mrs. Paddy went over to see what it was.

In the soft mud was a footprint, a big, almost round footprint.

In her eyes was a startled look as she exclaimed, "Puma the Cougar! Do you suppose he knows we are living here?"

Paddy grinned. "If he hasn't seen us he surely has seen this dam and this little pond. If he doesn't know what they mean he is stupid, and I never have heard him called that," said he.

Mrs. Paddy sighed. "With that fellow about it won't do for either of us to get more than a jump away from the water," said she. "It has been so lovely and peaceful here! Why must he come around to bother us now?"

"He hasn't bothered us yet," Paddy pointed out.

"He is bothering us this very minute," declared Mrs. Paddy. "That footprint bothers us because we know that it means danger. So we must be more careful and watchful than ever, and this when we have so much to do."

Paddy admitted that this was true. "But there is at least one thing we have to be thankful for," said he.

"I don't know what," retorted Mrs. Paddy. She was anxiously looking all around as if she expected Puma to step in sight any minute.

"That he didn't find out sooner that we are here. Now the pond, small as it is, still is big enough to give us safety. I wonder where the old killer is now. He may be watching us this very minute," replied Paddy.

Puma was. Yes, sir, he was doing just that. He was stretched out on a big limb of a tree from which he could look down on that little pond and its surroundings. He was watching the two workers with a hungry look in his fierce yellow eyes. Now and then he licked his lips.

"There are two good dinners," thought he. "Not that I need one of them just now, but I will later. It is a long time since I last tasted Beaver. Yes, sir, it is a very long time. A Beaver dinner is a good dinner." He licked his lips again.

"Those two are smart," he continued in silent talk to himself. "Yes, sir, they are smart. Only smart Beavers live to be as old as they are. I wonder if they have brought any young ones with them. Old Beaver is good eating, but young Beaver is better and easier to catch." Once more he licked his lips.

All the time Paddy and Mrs. Paddy, not knowing they were being watched, went about their work as if they did know. They were just as cautious, just as careful in everything they did as if they were fully aware that those fierce eyes were watching every move they made. They took no chances. Long ago they had learned that taking chances is never the way of wisdom.

It wasn't long before there was another hidden watcher at that little pond at the foot of the Great Mountain. It was Tufty the Lynx. Tufty has a tuft of quite long hairs springing from the tip of each ear, hence his name.

Furtive folk usually are those whose ways are ways of darkness — those who prefer night to day in order that their deeds may be unseen by others. They are soft-footed, moving about stealthily. As a rule the furtive folk of the Green Forest hunt and live on their smaller neighbors. Most members of the Cat family are furtive.

Alas, that so often relatives are bitter enemies, or at least are quarrelsome. It is so with Tufty the Lynx and his big cousin, Puma, who is also called Panther, Mountain Lion and sometimes Catamount. Neither has any kindly feeling for the other. One reason is that they are rivals. Both want the same things. Both are eaters of meat as Mother Nature made them to be. So both live by hunting the smaller Green Forest folk. The more difficult the hunting the more bitter becomes their feeling toward each other. Puma is the bigger, but in stealth and cunning Tufty is quite his equal.

Puma had been the first of the cousins to discover the new home of the Beavers. He had kept the discovery to himself, or tried to. But often it is easier to learn a thing than to keep it secret afterward. Anyway there was nothing really secret about that little pond growing bigger and bigger day by day. So it wasn't long before Tufty learned of it and began furtively to visit it every night, always trying to be unseen. That is his way of hunting.

On his very first visit his nose told him that his big cousin had been there. Knowing the ways of Puma he was sure the latter was doing just what he planned to do himself, watching those Beavers. Looking around for a tree from a limb of which he could overlook the dam and pond he came to the very tree

Puma was using. A warning growl greeted him. He snarled in return.

"Keep away from here. Those Beavers are mine," growled Puma.

"You haven't caught them. They are no more yours than mine," snarled Tufty.

"In so far as I can see they don't belong to either of you," said Hooty the Owl, who happened to be in the next tree.

Puma looked up and growled. Tufty looked up and snarled. Then they paid Hooty no more attention. For a long time Puma glared down at Tufty and Tufty glared up at his big cousin. Then Tufty seemed to melt into the darkness so silently did he slip away. A fight with his big cousin would be useless for Puma was too big and strong for him. An open quarrel would be just as useless. Indeed, it would be worse than useless for it would warn those Beavers that two of their most dangerous enemies were close at hand.

Of course he didn't know that they already knew it. Mrs. Paddy's keen nose had found Tufty's scent. As they already had found one of Puma's footprints they had no doubt at all that both cousins would be watching and waiting for a chance to catch one of them. But the rival cousins didn't know this. Both thought their presence was undiscovered, and each did his best to keep it so.

Paddy and Mrs. Paddy kept right on working, but with noses and ears always on guard. Of course they used their eyes too, but they depended little on these. They can hear far better and smell far better than they can see. The Merry Little Breezes by day, and the wandering Little Night Breezes in the darkness, brought them the scent that warned them that their enemies were near and just where they were. And as if to tease the two secret hunters the Breezes carried back to them the warm hunger-provoking Beaver scent.

So Paddy and Mrs. Paddy planned and worked, the furtive hunters planned and watched, the dam became longer and higher, the pond bigger and bigger, and the new home and community center grew and grew.

II. The Big House

Too often you will find it true
The critic talks but cannot do.
— PADDY THE BEAVER

QUEER AS IT MAY SEEM it is so. Folks who cannot do things themselves often appear to know more about how things should be done than those who do them. Anyway that is how it seems. The less they know about a matter the more ready they are to tell others what should or should not be done. The funny part of it all is that sometimes they are right.

Where folks are doing things you are sure to find others looking on. What is so fascinating in watching others work to those who do not work themselves I do not know, but so it is. It was so at the new pond in the Green Forest at the foot of the Great

Mountain. Night and day visitors came to look on. One of these was Mrs. Flathorns the Moose. She brought her twin calves there to drink.

They had watched the building of the dam. This they understood for they could see for themselves how it held back the water, making the pond. But the building of the house they didn't understand at all.

"It just doesn't make sense," declared Mother Flathorns to the twins. "Those folks are doing a lot of hard work with nothing to show for it. It looks foolish to me."

It would seem that way to one who knew nothing about building a house, particularly such a house as Paddy and Mrs. Paddy were building out in the water. At first all that those looking on could see was that the two workers kept bringing sticks and brush to a certain place and there disappearing under water with them. When the divers came up whatever they had brought was left on the bottom of the pond. It was this that didn't make sense to Mrs. Flathorns. It didn't make sense to Puma the Cougar or to Tufty the Lynx. It didn't make sense to Hooty the Owl, who came around every evening just out of curiosity, or to Croaker the Raven, who managed to find some excuse for a daily visit there.

"If they want to get rid of those sticks why don't they just drag them ashore?" croaked the big cousin of Blacky the Crow. But as no one else was around and he was merely talking to himself the question was unanswered.

12

Meanwhile the busy home builders paid no attention to those looking on save to make very sure that neither Puma nor Tufty should have a chance for a Beaver dinner. They continued to bring material and take it down under water at that one place. To judge by the muddiness of the water just there they were also doing a lot of digging on the bottom. It was all very perplexing to those who could not see what actually was being done down there under water even though it was not deep there.

At last sticks and brush began to show above the surface of the water. More sticks and more brush were brought and piled on top. Some of the sticks were long poles from which the bark had been peeled and probably eaten. Mud was brought up and added.

Croaker the Raven cocked his head on one side, trying to look wise. Just why holding one's head to one side should be thought to indicate wisdom I do not know, but so it is.

"They are building an island," declared Croaker. "I can see that now. Clever folks, those Beavers. I suppose they want a place to sit where they can feel perfectly safe. It is a lot of hard work. Perhaps it is worth it, but I doubt it. Nothing would be worth all that work to me. They must want an island badly." He cocked his head to the other side, but looked no wiser than before.

Paddy and Mrs. Paddy paid no attention to such remarks if they overheard. They went about their business as folks who know just what they are doing always do. Presently they had

what appeared to be a small island and nothing more. On the side toward the middle of the pond the water was deeper than on the opposite side and was being made deeper still by the digging of mud from the bottom. This was added to the island.

"A lot of foolish work when they could just as well sit on their dam when they want to rest," said the onlookers.

Tufty the Lynx was one of these. Keeping well hidden he

spent a lot of time watching. It wasn't because he was at all interested in the work. Not the least bit. He was watching for opportunity.

"If you don't watch for opportunity you are pretty sure to miss it when it comes your way," says Tufty. Of course he is right. What was the opportunity he was watching for? To get a dinner, of course, a dinner of toothsome Beaver freshly caught. He liked less and less what he saw. If that island was being made to rest on instead of the dam his likelihood of opportunity was growing less as the island grew bigger.

It was Mrs. Paddy who had chosen the place for the new house. Paddy approved her choice of location. Long ago he had learned that in such a matter it was best to allow Mrs. Paddy to have her own way without argument because in the end she would have it anyway. There are many folks who could profit by following Paddy's example. However, in this instance he would have chosen that very place himself. The only thing he questioned was the size of the house. It seemed to him that Mrs. Paddy was planning too big a house, altogether too big a house.

"My dear," said he, "there are but two of us."

"So what?" asked Mrs. Paddy.

"It looks to me as if you are planning a house big enough for a dozen. Yes, my dear, that is how it looks to me," replied Paddy good-naturedly.

"Even so, what of it?" Mrs. Paddy wanted to know.

"Only that we have a lot to do and not much time to do it in.

A smaller house would take less time and less work to build. As I said before, there are but two of us. It seems to me that in building such a big house we will be wasting time, and time is important. Much work is still to be done on the dam. The pond isn't yet as big as it should be. And you know we haven't even begun the food pile," replied Paddy.

"It is easier to build now than it will be to rebuild next year. You seem to have forgotten that

> Children come and children grow.
> We must provide for them, you know.

I don't believe in doing things only for the present when it is possible to plan ahead. In the building of a home we should always plan ahead," retorted Mrs. Paddy.

"Perhaps you are right," Paddy admitted a bit ruefully.

"I know I am. There is no perhaps about it," declared Mrs. Paddy. "Too small a house is a poor start for a good home." She slapped the water with her big flat tail just by way of showing that she meant what she said.

Paddy grinned and said no more. "Her mind is made up and that is all there is to it," he thought philosophically and forthwith entered into the work of building that new house as enthusiastically as if he fully agreed with Mrs. Paddy as to the size it should be.

By now the pond was really big enough and deep enough to be called a pond. At first the water had leaked through the dam freely. They were not big leaks but there were many of them. However, as more and more drift stuff — twigs, fallen leaves and other things — was brought down by Laughing Brook and lodged against the dam many of the leaks were gradually plugged. Of course Paddy and Mrs. Paddy kept adding sticks and mud and sometimes small logs and stones. They dug out turf along the foot of the dam and added this. The tighter the dam became, of course, the more water it held back and the larger the pond became.

It wasn't until she was sure that the pond was big enough, and at the place she had chosen the water was deep enough, that Mrs. Paddy started work on the house itself. Then she gave all her attention to it. She and Paddy worked as if their lives depended on how soon they got that house built. Perhaps they did. If Jack Frost should come extra early and cover the pond with ice before the house was ready for them to live in, and before they had time to build a big enough pile of food sticks, they would be in trouble indeed.

Paddy still felt that the house would be much bigger than necessary but said nothing. There wasn't time for argument. So presently there appeared above the surface of the water what their neighbors mistook for just an island. It was an island, but it was much more. It was the foundation of a fine big house.

III. Hurry and Worry

Always folks who have to hurry
Are the ones most prone to worry.
— PADDY THE BEAVER

THE NEW HOUSE rose high out of water, a great rounded pile of poles and shorter sticks and mud, sloping from the top to the water's edge. "Paddy's folly," it was called by Croaker the Raven. More than once he had flown over and lighted on it, looking it over thoroughly.

"It is nothing but a mass of sticks and mud," he declared. "Those Beavers call it a house, but a house is a place to go into and live in. No one can go into that pile of stuff. It hasn't a room in it. It wasn't built right. Imagine building a house you can't

18

get into! That is what those silly Beavers have done. I had always supposed they were smart, but I've changed my mind."

Croaker made fun of Paddy and Mrs. Paddy whenever he got a chance. They didn't appear to mind. They were constantly busy about the new house, though just what they were doing no one seemed to know. They kept plunging down close to the house where the water was deepest, keeping it muddy. Bits of wood floated to the surface.

"What are you doing down there — trying to get in?" asked Croaker. He chuckled in a deep coarse voice.

"We are minding our own business, which is more than can be said for some others," retorted Paddy. He plunged below just as Mrs. Paddy came up.

Croaker had thought it a joke when he had asked Paddy if he was trying to get in that house, but if there was a joke it was on Croaker, not on Paddy. He and Mrs. Paddy *were* trying to get in. What is more they were getting in. Down at the bottom of the pond they were digging and cutting an underwater passage right into that island they had first built for a foundation.

That passage was planned with care. It led in and up until it opened on what had been the surface of the island before walls and roof were begun. Before beginning the latter they had built a mound of mud on the middle of the island. On this they had leaned long poles, the rafters of the roof. Now from below they dug away all that mound of mud, taking it out through the new hall. When all was out a nice large dry room was left where

19

the mound had been. It could be reached only from underwater. No one but themselves knew of it. So you see the joke really was on Croaker.

Croaker is big and bold. He dresses all in black. His coat looks as if it might have been cut from the midnight blackness of a cloudy night. He is much like his cousin, Blacky the Crow, only much bigger. His voice is harsher. Of all the folks in feathers and fur who live on the Great Mountain, or in the Green Forest at the base of it, Croaker is given the credit of being one of the smartest and shrewdest.

But even the smartest folks sometimes are fooled, and the keenest wits are without knowledge in some matters. It was so with Croaker in his judgment of Paddy and Mrs. Paddy. When they had started to build their house out in the water he had thought them very clever to build it where it could be reached only by swimming or flying. Yes, indeed, he had thought them very clever. Then he had changed his opinion and thought them very stupid. He said so. Had he not watched them build a great solid pile of sticks and mud and call it a house? A house must have at least one room and this had none. He knew because he had been on hand every day to watch it built.

"I didn't suppose anyone would be so stupid as to do a thing like that. Had I not seen it with my own eyes I wouldn't have believed it," he would say. Then he would chuckle hoarsely.

Now Croaker is canny. Yes, sir, he is canny, which is another way of saying that he is really smart. He always has his wits

about him. He knows that the cleverest people do at times make mistakes. So after a day or two of hoarse chuckling he stopped. His keen eyes miss little and he had taken note that Paddy and Mrs. Paddy were spending much time under water close to the house, taking turns. He didn't miss the muddy water and the chips of wood floating to the surface.

"What are you folks doing down there under water?" he demanded of Paddy when he got the chance.

"Finishing our house," replied Paddy, and said no more.

It was then that Croaker knew that the joke was on him after all. He guessed that somehow an entrance and room were being made. He wouldn't have admitted it, but as a fact he was beginning to have something very like respect for his neighbors with the flat tails. He was smart and smart folks usually respect other smart folks.

Have you ever noticed how often hurry and worry go together? Perhaps it isn't always true, but as a general rule it is. Folks in a hurry seem bound to worry, and the greater the hurry the more the worry.

Paddy the Beaver isn't given to much worrying. He isn't like Peter Rabbit who looks behind him more than he looks ahead, and so is forever running into trouble. Paddy looks ahead and plans things to avoid this. But there is none who does not at some time worry. So it was now with Paddy and Mrs. Paddy.

The house was practically completed. There was still some work to be done inside, ends of projecting sticks in the living room to be gnawed off and perhaps a little enlarging to be done, but these things could wait. They could be done later. The thing now was to get enough food to last all winter, and time was short. This was because it had taken so long to build that big house. It made them late starting the harvest.

Hardly had this begun when Paddy began to worry, and of course Mrs. Paddy worried too. Nights were colder than was usual at this time in the fall. Even the days were cooler than might be expected. Honker the Goose on his way south from the Far North, where he had spent the summer, spied the new pond and with his flock dropped in to spend a night. He brought news, disturbing news. Jack Frost had started south early this year and unless he lingered on the way he would arrive ahead of his usual time. That was why Honker was leading his flock south earlier than usual.

"Now we *will* have to hurry. We mustn't waste a minute. If this pond should be frozen over before we have completed our food pile we shall be in trouble, the very worst kind of trouble," declared Paddy.

Mrs. Paddy nodded. "If that should happen I don't know what we would do. What could we do? You don't think it will happen, do you?" she asked anxiously.

"How should I know?" replied Paddy a bit shortly. "You know as much about it as I do. Of one thing we may be sure and this is that from now on we work night and day."

That is what they did. Yes, sir, they did just that. Day and

23

night they worked, sometimes together and sometimes alone. They took time from work only to eat and for such sleep as they had to have. It was hurry, hurry all the time, and worry, worry, worry much of the time. From long experience and what they had seen happen to others they knew what a short supply of food might mean. Once the pond was covered with thick ice they would be prisoners. Even if there should be an open place it wouldn't be safe for them to go ashore in search of food. Very likely there would be deep snow. In that they would be helpless if surprised by a hungry enemy. They must have a food pile big enough to last them until spring. They *must*.

The moment the harvest began they had to be doubly watchful. The aspen and poplar trees to supply them with the bark that through the winter would be their only food must be cut down and then cut up into short lengths to be towed or pushed out to the food pile in the pond near the house. This cutting must be done on land. Puma the Cougar, Tufty the Lynx, Buster Bear and Old Man Coyote knew this and would take every advantage of the fact. Just one careless moment of forgetfulness might cost the life of Paddy or Mrs. Paddy. They must keep ever watchful while they worked on land. Only in the water were they safe.

"We will cut only those trees close to the water. Luckily there are plenty of them," said Paddy.

So this was what they did. The food pile grew slowly. The nights grew colder. Paddy and Mrs. Paddy hurried and worried.

IV. Buster Bear Loses Face

A swift retreat is no disgrace
When odds are much too great to face.

— BUSTER BEAR

ALREADY THE NEW POND had become a community center. Some came to drink and to bathe. Some came to see who else was there. Some came out of idle curiosity. Flathorns the Moose had come often. He always seemed to be looking for someone. Of all those who visited the pond he was the biggest.

Just now in the early evening he was standing at the edge of the pond with his front feet in the water. He was looking at his own reflection and he was filled with pride. He tipped his head this way and studied the reflection. He tipped his head that way

25

and studied the reflection. What he saw pleased him greatly. "Never before have I had such a crown," thought he admiringly.

Again he tipped his head, first this way, then that way, that he might better see and admire the great antlers on his head. They were something to see, something to be proud of. Indeed they were. Flathorns was proud of them. They made him look as if he might in truth be what some folks called him, King of the Forest.

Paddy and Mrs. Paddy looked at him admiringly. "He looks better than I ever have seen him before," said Paddy. "Just look at those great antlers that some folks call horns! He swings them about as if they were nothing at all. He doesn't look or act much as he did when I was up this way early in the summer. Then he had no antlers. He was thin and poor and looked as if he might run from his own shadow. Now look at him! He looks as if he is fairly aching to try those great antlers in a fight."

"And to think he grew those great things on his head in just one summer!" exclaimed Mrs. Paddy.

Paddy nodded. "He grew them the same way Lightfoot the Deer grows his each summer," said he. "How such hard things can grow just like a plant I can't understand. Mother Nature does many wonderful things but to me this is one of the most wonderful. In the summer he acted as if he were ashamed to be seen. It didn't seem right for such a great fellow to be so timid. Now he isn't afraid of anybody."

"I wonder what he would do if he should meet Buster Bear," said Mrs. Paddy.

Paddy chuckled. "I know what would happen," said he.

"What?" asked Mrs. Paddy.

"Buster would run away or climb a tree. Big as he is he doesn't want trouble with Flathorns as he is now," said Paddy.

Meanwhile Flathorns was rubbing his great antlers on the trunk of a tree. From one side he had rubbed off all the bark to a considerable height. He was polishing the points. Presently he began thrashing about in the brush, making a great noise. He pawed the ground, digging into it with his front hoofs. He was in high spirits, glorying in his own strength. He was showing off just for his own satisfaction and for the benefit of any others who, like Paddy and Mrs. Paddy, might be looking on.

Perhaps Flathorns was hoping that Mrs. Flathorns might be watching him. He knew that if she was it would be from hiding. She wouldn't show herself but would make him look for her. If a rival should appear she would make him fight for her. He wanted to fight. He wished a rival would appear. Then he could show his might. Only in this way could he prove his right to go where he pleased and do what he pleased. It is like this with some of the nations of the earth, and because of it all the world must suffer.

Flathorns stopped showing off. He came down to the water and waded out. He drank deeply. Then he waded right across the pond. Having such long legs he could do this with no trouble at all. Had the water been deep enough he would have crossed by swimming. He is a very good swimmer. He made the water muddy. The two owners of the pond didn't like that.

When he left the water on the other side he disappeared among the trees as quietly as he had been noisy a short time before.

Mistress Moon had climbed above the tops of the trees and was making open places almost as light as by day. The Black Shadows had stolen out across part of the pond. Beyond them it gleamed like silver. Paddy had climbed out on the roof of his house to rest for a moment or two. He had just towed a large stick to the food pile. It was hard work. Presently he heard someone coming toward the pond, not trying to be quiet about it.

"Buster Bear," thought Paddy. "He must be feeling good and doesn't care who hears him."

Buster was feeling good. It was the time of year when he feels his best. All summer he had had good living. There had been a wonderful crop of berries. Buster loves berries. He is really piggish when he gets in a good berry patch. A big crop of beechnuts and acorns had followed and Buster loves both. He had had a full stomach most of the time. He is always happy when he has a full stomach, wherein he is like many other people.

Since Buster is so big and so strong he has the respect of most of his neighbors. When they see his great claws they are careful not to get too near and not to interfere with him in any way. Now it isn't a good thing for anyone never to be interfered with. It too often gives them a wrong idea of their own importance. They get to thinking that they can do what they please, when they please and as they please. They forget that others have equal rights. It was so with Buster Bear.

He liked to see the smaller folks hurriedly get out of his way. It made him feel important and he liked the feeling. Most folks do. It had reached a point where he expected everybody to step aside for him, to show him respect and perhaps admiration.

So for a long time Buster had been coming and going about as he pleased. He paid little attention to anyone, not even Puma the Cougar whom many call Mountain Lion. When their paths chanced to cross one night Buster merely said, "Woof, woof," way down deep in his throat.

"Gr-r-r-r-r-r," replied Puma, also way down deep in his throat. Then each went on his own way.

Careless of who saw or heard him Buster was coming to Paddy's pond for a drink. He wasn't bothering to look around. Even if he had looked he might not have seen Flathorns standing perfectly still in the midst of the Black Shadows where they had crowded together and were blackest. Although his coat isn't black he appeared as black as they were. Right then there was no fear in him, not even the fear of Man. Nowhere in the Green Forest was there anyone Flathorns feared to meet.

Just a little way from him Buster Bear stepped out in the moonlight. Somehow he always looks bigger in moonlight than in sunlight. He stopped and stood up on his hind legs like a Man. He stood perfectly still.

"If I didn't know better I might think him to be a big, tall, black stump," thought Paddy, watching from the roof of his house out in the water.

A wandering Little Night Breeze danced past Flathorns, carrying a little of the Moose scent over to Buster Bear. Buster didn't like that smell. No, sir, he didn't like it at all. He growled way down deep in his throat. It was an ugly growl, a threatening growl. He drew back his lips to show his big teeth. Paddy could see them white in the moonlight.

Buster wasn't afraid. Not just then anyway. He was undecided what to do, whether to go on or to turn back and quietly go away. It wasn't fear. He just didn't want trouble, that was all.

More than once during the summer he had met Flathorns and Flathorns had moved out of his way. He was growing new antlers then and they were soft and tender and in the growing of them he had lost much strength. So he had avoided having trouble with Buster Bear. Buster was remembering this now. It was what made him undecided. He couldn't make up his mind whether to keep on or go back.

"I do believe he isn't afraid of anybody any more than Flathorns is," thought Paddy admiringly.

And then it happened. There was a grunting snort and a heavy crash in the brush. Out plunged Flathorns, his head lowered, his great antlers pointing straight at Buster Bear. Buster was no longer undecided. His mind was made up for him. He climbed a tree and he climbed in a hurry.

"Huh!" exclaimed Paddy the Beaver, and if you had heard him you would have known that Buster Bear had lost face, as is said of those who have lost the good opinion of others.

V. Up a Tree

Be careful when you climb a tree
That to get down you're wholly free.
— BUSTER BEAR

BUSTER BEAR had lost face with Paddy the Beaver. Paddy no longer thought Buster important and unafraid of anybody and so to be envied. Only a few minutes ago he had thought it would be wonderful to be like Buster, afraid of no one. Then out had charged Flathorns; Buster had taken one look at the points of the great antlers coming straight at him and hadn't waited to find out what they felt like. Right then he wanted to get beyond the reach of Flathorns, in the quickest way possible, and he did. He climbed a tree. You know he is a very good

31

climber. Big as he is he went up that tree in a way that would have been a credit to Happy Jack Squirrel. It was right then that Buster lost face with Paddy. He hadn't even tried to fight.

"Huh!" exclaimed Paddy. "He's afraid. He is just as much afraid as I would be. If I were as big as he is and had such big claws and teeth I wouldn't be afraid of anybody."

It was true that Buster had been afraid. But he wasn't now. He had been a badly frightened Bear until he got his claws into the bark of that tree. Then he was no longer afraid. He could climb and Flathorns couldn't. He knew he had done just the right thing. Had he run the big Moose would soon have caught up with him for Flathorns could run faster than he could. But now he was safe with nothing to worry about. He would make himself comfortable up there in that tree and wait until Flathorns went away.

He didn't climb to the top of the tree as he would have had he been a cub. He was too big for that. He made himself comfortable on a big limb just high enough to be out of reach of Flathorns when he stood up and slashed at him with the sharp-edged hoofs of his front feet.

Flathorns was in a terrible temper. He snorted. He grunted. He pawed the ground. He slashed surrounding brush with his great antlers. He walked round and round the tree in which Buster was now quite comfortable. He dared Buster to come down.

Buster didn't. Of course not. The truth is he was rather enjoying the affair. But after a long time he became tired of staying up in that tree and wanted to get down. He couldn't. Flathorns still kept guard below. Buster was a prisoner in that tree.

At long, long last Flathorns disappeared where the Black Shadows were blackest. Buster waited. He watched. He listened. At last when he was sure that it was safe to go down he started down backward as is the way of a Bear in a tree. He was as quiet about it as he could be, but he couldn't help making some noise. He had reached a place where he was just about ready to let go and drop when there was a crash and a grunt. Out plunged Flathorns. You should have seen Buster climb then!

Twice the same thing was repeated. Buster lost patience. He was becoming peeved. He hadn't expected to be kept a prisoner. He wondered how long Flathorns would keep him up there. He growled — deep, rumbly, grumbly growls that had the ugliest sound you can imagine. He told Flathorns what he would do to him if he should come down. This made Flathorns more furious than ever.

Of course Buster had no intention of going down. He would stay right where he was even if it should mean all night and all the next day. After a while he got over his anger and began feeling sorry for himself. Here he was a prisoner for no reason at all but that Flathorns was full of fight and had no one else to fight with. It wasn't fair.

"Come on down and fight!" snorted the big Moose.

33

"I don't want to fight," whined Buster.

Flathorns made no reply. I suspect he was getting even for the times when, without antlers, he had to step aside for Buster. You know sometimes there is a lot of satisfaction in getting even. It isn't a nice thing to do. But it is satisfying.

When finally Flathorns left and went off up the mountain he did it so quietly that Buster didn't know he had gone.

Now having seen Buster Bear afraid Paddy the Beaver had lost respect for him. Somehow all of us lose respect for those whom we have feared when we see them afraid themselves.

"That fellow isn't so much," said Paddy to Mrs. Paddy. "If I were his size and had such great claws and teeth as he has I wouldn't be afraid of anyone. I wouldn't run away from Flat-horns or anyone else. I would make everybody run from me."

Only a few nights later Paddy was cutting down a tree. He had it cut half through, prying out big chips with his great orange-colored cutting teeth. There was a sound much like the report of a gun. Paddy didn't even turn his head to look around. He scrambled for the water and plunged in. Safety first is his watchword. It is a wise watchword for you and me. That report had been made by Mrs. Paddy's broad, thick tail slapping the water hard. It meant danger. Paddy swam under water and came up right beside Mrs. Paddy.

"What is it?" he whispered. Of course he meant the danger.

"Puma," whispered Mrs. Paddy.

"Where?" asked Paddy, still whispering.

"Behind the log just back of that tree at which you were working. I saw him just in time," replied Mrs. Paddy.

"I'm glad you did, my dear," whispered Paddy as he looked over to the place where he had been at work.

Just then Mistress Moon came out from behind a cloud. She flooded that spot with soft, silvery light. Then Paddy saw Puma. He fears no one more than he does the big Mountain Lion.

35

Puma slowly rose to his feet. He drew back his lips in a snarl. He walked to the edge of the water, lashing his tail. He was in a rage with disappointment. At that very instant Buster Bear walked out into the moonlight a little way from Puma.

Buster stopped. Puma faced him and crouched, the tip of his long tail twitching as the tails of all Cats have a way of doing. He showed his teeth. Paddy and Mrs. Paddy could see them gleam in the moonlight. It made them shiver.

"Buster will run now," whispered Paddy.

Buster didn't run. He held his ground. He didn't back so much as one step. In his turn he drew back his lips and showed all his teeth. They gleamed in the moonlight. Again Paddy and Mrs. Paddy shivered, and it wasn't because they were cold.

Puma snarled. Buster Bear growled. Puma, crouched close to the ground, worked forward a little. Under him he drew his strong hind feet in position to spring. The two Beavers held their breath.

Buster Bear didn't move. He stood right there growling. It had an ugly sound. Never had he sounded uglier. Puma continued to crouch and snarl, twitching his tail. For what seemed a long time but really was only a moment or two, neither moved.

It was Buster who moved first and what he did wasn't at all what Paddy expected him to do. He didn't turn and run away. Instead of this he moved forward a step or two straight toward Puma.

For a moment Puma held his ground, snarling ugly threats. Then as Buster Bear, with the ugliest-sounding growl the two watchers ever had heard, came on Puma suddenly turned and began to sneak away. He was still snarling angrily, but he was leaving. He had turned tail and was sneaking away. In a moment he had disappeared. Buster Bear came down to the water and began to drink.

Paddy looked at Mrs. Paddy. Mrs. Paddy looked at Paddy. "Did you see what I saw?" asked Paddy. Mrs. Paddy nodded.

So it was that Buster Bear recovered face with Paddy the Beaver and ever since has been regarded with respect.

VI. The Love Call

Suspicion is a hateful thing,
Yet it alone may safety bring.
— FLATHORNS THE MOOSE

LOVE OFTEN FINDS expression in teasing the loved ones.
Mrs. Flathorns was teasing Flathorns by keeping out of his
sight, but taking care that he should know that she wasn't far
away. If he went too far looking for her she would call him back
with her love call. Hearing it for the first time you wouldn't
guess that it was a love call. No one but a Moose would. To
other ears it is neither loving nor lovely.

In the pride of his strength and his great spreading antlers
Flathorns feared no one and came and went as he pleased, and

38

was admired by all his Green Forest neighbors. Other eyes saw him and they, too, looked with admiration and with something more. It was desire.

"That is the biggest Moose and those are the biggest antlers I ever have seen. I want that head and I mean to have it to put on the wall of my office when the hunting season opens," declared the owner of those eyes.

It was a short time later that Paddy and Mrs. Paddy became uneasy. It wasn't that they were unused to having visitors. They were not. Their pond probably had more visitors than any other place in all the Green Forest round about. You remember that it was a community center. Mrs. Lightfoot the Deer brought her slender-legged, pretty twins there daily to drink. Buster Bear came often. Flathorns came almost every night and more than once Paddy had seen Mrs. Flathorns watching him admiringly from a thicket on the opposite shore. Old Man Coyote dropped around now and then. So did Tufty the Lynx and Puma the Cougar. Yes, Paddy and Mrs. Paddy were used to visitors and seldom disturbed by them.

But twice lately there had been other visitors, visitors who walked upright on two legs and whom all the Green Forest folk hated with the hatred that is born of distrust and fear. They came in the daytime and spent much time looking along the shore. They found many footprints, among them the big ones of Flathorns.

"Those were made by that big fellow we want and they show

that he comes here often. This is the place for us," said one of the hunters and the other agreed.

"They didn't do us any harm," said Mrs. Paddy as she and Paddy watched the two out of sight.

"Not this time, but that doesn't mean they won't next time. They'll be back," said Paddy.

"How do you know?" asked Mrs. Paddy.

"Don't ask me how I know; I just *know*. It is a feeling, my dear, and it almost never fails to be right," replied Paddy.

"Anyway they didn't see us," said Mrs. Paddy.

"That may be," agreed Paddy, "but it doesn't mean anything. Long ago I learned to expect trouble for someone whenever those two-legged folks are about. They'll be back. Just wait and see."

Of course Paddy was right. It was a little before dark the very next evening that the two hunters returned. Well hidden themselves, Paddy and Mrs. Paddy watched with growing suspicion. For a short time the two hunters were very busy about something a little back from the shore. Just what they were doing couldn't be seen from where Paddy and Mrs. Paddy were watching. They were very quiet and presently they disappeared.

Had they gone away? The two Beavers wished they had some means of knowing. For a long time they floated in the water in the shadow of their big house watching and listening. They saw nothing and heard nothing of the late visitors to their pond yet their uneasy feeling grew.

Jolly, round, red Mr. Sun disappeared behind the trees, going down to bed behind the Purple Hills just as Paddy and Mrs. Paddy had watched him do countless times before. The rosy glow he left behind slowly faded. The Black Shadows hurried out to wrap the shores in darkness. One by one the stars appeared and twinkled down at their reflections in the still water of the pond. Their reflections twinkled back at them. The hush of perfect peace settled over all the Green Forest.

"I wish I knew where those two-legged ones are," thought Paddy.

No ripple disturbed the glassy surface of the pond. It was so still that it seemed as if Mother Nature was holding her breath. The soft light of Mistress Moon crept through the tops of the trees and soon flooded down from above them, silvering the surface of the little pond. It seemed as if in that lovely peaceful scene there could be no ugly thing. Yet there was. It was suspicion. Suspicion always is ugly though often necessary.

Paddy and Mrs. Paddy felt it. Something was wrong, but what it was they didn't know. They just felt it.

At last the silence was broken. "Who-hoo-hoo-hoo-hooo!" sounded the voice of Hooty the Great Horned Owl. It was his hunting call. He was far away but in that perfect stillness he sounded close at hand. It didn't disturb the two watchers. They were too big for Hooty to even think of bothering.

A few minutes later from nearby there came a sound so loud that it fairly shattered the silence. It rang through the Green Forest and was echoed back from the Great Mountain. It was so startling that it made the two Beavers jump although they knew instantly what it was. It was a harsh, discordant sound with no sweetness or softness in it. Had you been there, not knowing what it was, I am sure you would never have even dreamed that it had anything to do with love. Yet there was in it a suggestion of loneliness, of yearning and longing.

Paddy looked at Mrs. Paddy, then both looked over at the shore. "Mrs. Flathorns," whispered Paddy. "That is her love call. I wonder if Flathorns heard it."

"If he didn't there surely is something the matter with his ears," whispered Mrs. Paddy.

They listened for a reply, but heard none. Again stillness wrapped the Green Forest. For long it was unbroken. Then once more that bellowing love call rang through the Green Forest.

"It is from the wrong side of the pond," whispered Paddy. There was suspicion in his whisper.

"What do you mean?" whispered Mrs. Paddy.

"Mrs. Flathorns never comes to the water on that side. We always have seen her on the other shore. Remember?" replied Paddy.

Before Mrs. Paddy could reply there came a startling sound from the foot of the Great Mountain. It was a grunt, a deep heavy grunt. It was followed by a sound as if someone, a very big someone, was crashing through brush and bushes.

"Flathorns!" whispered Paddy. "He heard that call and is coming and doesn't care who knows it."

Paddy started to swim around close to the other shore. Mrs. Paddy was close behind. They floated where the Black Shadows lay heaviest on the water. From their midst they could look over to the opposite shore. Again came that love call but not so loud this time. Again Flathorns grunted a reply and they could hear him crashing through the undergrowth in the distance. He seemed to be coming recklessly to that call.

But after a few minutes they heard no further sound from him. Was he still coming, or wasn't he? The fact is Flathorns had suddenly become suspicious. He stood for many minutes listening. When he did start on he took care to make no sound. He moved with the silence of a great black shadow. Why was he suspicious? He didn't know. Perhaps there was a note in that last call that didn't seem quite right. Perhaps it was just a feeling, nothing more. He held his big nose high, hoping a Little Night Breeze would come from the pond bringing the scent of Mrs. Flathorns if she were there. None did. All the Little Night Breezes were asleep. There was not one to take to him the scent of the two hunters hidden where they could watch the shore of the pond.

Paddy turned to look at the shore behind him. He nudged Mrs. Paddy. She turned and looked. There, a black shadow among lighter shadows, stood Mrs. Flathorns. Just then there was a low coaxing call. It wasn't from Mrs. Flathorns. It was from the opposite shore.

VII. A Slap in Time

None is so independent he
Is from all obligations free.
— OLD MOTHER NATURE

AT ONE PLACE on the opposite shore Paddy could see that the Black Shadows had gathered until it seemed as if the darkness there might be felt. It was as if they were trying to hide something or someone in their midst. It was from that darkest place that low coaxing call had come and the other calls before it.

Flathorns was somewhere near. Paddy and Mrs. Paddy were sure of it. They had heard him grunt in the distance. They had heard him rattle his great antlers against a tree. They had heard

45

him crashing through brush, careless of who might hear him. But for some time there had been no sound from him. Did it mean that he had become suspicious that not all was as it should be? Was that the reason for that low coaxing love call?

But the two Beavers knew now that something was wrong. It wasn't Mrs. Flathorns who had called. They knew this now for a certainty. Even as they heard that last call they had seen Mrs. Flathorns, a dark shadow among lighter shadows, on the shore behind them. That call was from the opposite shore. Mrs. Flathorns had made no sound. Could it be she had a rival?

Now came a low grunt. It seemed to come from only a little way back in the woods. Then all was still again. Paddy swam slowly over to the shore where Flathorns was. He was curious. He wanted to see that other Moose whose calls had brought Flathorns down from the Great Mountain. He was careful to make no sound as slowly he swam close to shore. He made hardly a ripple. When he was opposite the darkest place he floated. Like other night-loving folk he has eyes for seeing in the night, but not when it is too dark. None of them can see in complete darkness any more than you or I can.

He still had that feeling that something was not as it should be. Indeed, it was stronger than ever. It filled him with uneasiness. Call it suspicion, for of course this is what it really was. As he floated there staring at that dark place he grew more uneasy. Why? He couldn't say.

The stillness could almost be felt. For quite a while it was broken only by the distant hooting of Hooty as he hunted for his dinner. It was so still there around that little pond deep in the Green Forest that had you been there you would, I am sure, have thought there was no one else in all the neighborhood round about. Yet somewhere not far away in the darkness was the largest of all the Green Forest people, Flathorns the Moose. And right at the edge of the water on the other side of the little pond was Mrs. Flathorns. And in that darkest place so very near was the maker of those love calls.

Who was it? Four people were wondering. Flathorns was wondering. He had supposed it was Mrs. Flathorns, but now for no real reason he wasn't sure. Mrs. Flathorns was wondering. Could it be that she had a rival for the affections of Flathorns? The very thought made her bristle with jealousy. Paddy and Mrs. Paddy were wondering, knowing that it wasn't Mrs. Flathorns.

A small stick snapped in the darkness. It was a very faint sound, but Paddy heard it. He has very good ears. They are better and more to be trusted than his eyes. He knew that there in the darkest place someone had moved. Someone must have to have snapped that little stick. A ray of moonlight crept into the darkest part of that darkest place. It found and touched something that glimmered ever so faintly. There should be nothing there that would glimmer even ever so faintly. Paddy stared harder than ever. Someone in there had moved.

Slap! That was Paddy's big, flat, thick tail hitting the surface of the water. It was so wholly unexpected and so loud that it was startling. Even Mrs. Paddy, who was used to that sound, jumped. It was Paddy's danger signal. All the Green Forest people know and understand it. It was a warning to Mrs. Paddy that there might be danger near. It meant the same thing to others who heard it. Even as his tail hit the water Paddy plunged under.

Long ago Paddy had learned the value of quick action. If he suspects danger he acts first and finds out about it later. If he finds that he was mistaken, that there was no real danger, he doesn't mind. He calls it a good mistake as, of course, it is. You know there can be good mistakes as well as bad ones.

Says Paddy, "It is better to make many good mistakes than just one bad one," and he lives accordingly. Good mistakes never get one into trouble.

That slap on the water had sounded in the stillness as loud as and very like a rifle shot. As Paddy and Mrs. Paddy plunged under water there was a loud crash in the darkness a little way back in the woods. It was Flathorns leaving in a hurry and caring not at all how much noise he made as he plunged through the brush, breaking down small trees that were in his way. He meant to get away from there, and quick. Over on the other side of the little pond Mrs. Flathorns left almost as hurriedly, but with hardly a sound. And from where the Black Shadows were blackest two hunters stepped out into the moonlight.

"Confound that Beaver!" exclaimed one. "But for him we would have had that Moose. One more call like that last one would have brought him out into the moonlight. I am sure it was that big fellow we have seen in this neighborhood. He has the finest head of antlers I have ever seen. I don't suppose it will be of any use to do any more calling tonight."

"Not a bit," replied the other. In his hand he held a horn of birch bark. It was with this he had been imitating the love calls of Mrs. Flathorns. "Old Flathorns won't be fooled a second time. You may be sure of that," he continued. "If you are to get him you will have to do it by hunting, not by calling. To be honest I am glad we failed. I don't like this calling business."

"Why not?" the other asked. "It takes as much skill to fool a Moose by calling as it does to still-hunt him, and you are the best caller I ever have heard. You talk real Moose love talk with that birch-bark horn of yours."

"That's the trouble," replied the other. "It *is* love talk, and it is just plain treachery, nothing less. To call a noble great animal to his death by making him think it is his mate who is calling him isn't sport. It is just plain treachery. That is why I am glad that Beaver saved old Flathorns. That is why I think I will never call another Moose except for fun. It *is* fun, you know, to fool a wary old Moose by talking to him in his own language. Calling Moose to be shot is outlawed in many places and should be everywhere. Any way you look at it it is the very worst kind of treachery. So I'm through with it from this night on."

The other grinned a bit ruefully. "I never have given the matter much thought. You may be right, Jim," said he. "I

49

guess I have thought more about getting that head for a trophy than I have about the way I might get it. From now on we will still-hunt and cut out the calling."

From behind their house in the water Paddy and Mrs. Paddy watched the two hunters start off on their way back to their camp. "I knew something was wrong and I was right. I felt it, but I didn't know what it was," said Paddy.

"Well, you know now, and it is high time for us to get back to work," replied Mrs. Paddy. She started swimming toward the place where they had been cutting food trees and Paddy followed.

Flathorns did not return that night, nor did Mrs. Flathorns. But early the following evening Flathorns came to the pond for a drink. He moved carefully and silently until he was where he could see Paddy swimming with a big aspen stick to add to the food pile. Then he knew there was no danger, nothing to fear, and came boldly down to the water's edge.

"Thank you for giving me the danger signal last night," said he.

"I didn't give *you* the signal. It was for Mrs. Paddy," replied Paddy.

"That may be, but it probably saved my life. So thanks just the same," grunted the big Moose.

"Don't mention it. I'm always glad to help my neighbors," replied Paddy and went on to the food pile.

VIII. The Grunting Challenge

Who loudest boasts about his might
May thus be masking fear to fight.
— OLD MOTHER NATURE

IT WAS a clear still night, so cool as to be almost cold. Paddy and Mrs. Paddy were working as only Beavers can and will when there is work that must be done in a hurry. The food pile for the winter was almost big enough. It might even be made to do should Jack Frost arrive unexpectedly and cover the pond with ice. Paddy was cutting down a tree. Mrs. Paddy was trimming the branches from one she already had felled. It was a quiet peaceful scene.

Once far away Hooty the Owl called. Then for a long time

nothing was to be heard but such sounds as were made by the busy workers, and these were faint. Mistress Moon had climbed high in the sky and was flooding the pond and the surrounding Green Forest with her soft light. It was very beautiful and wonderfully peaceful on and around that little pond at the foot of the Great Mountain. Not a single mischievous Little Night Breeze was stirring. There was nothing to suggest that anywhere in all the region round about were any folks other than the busy workers trying so hard to beat Jack Frost.

Suddenly, without the slightest warning, the deep silence was broken by a sound so loud, so startling, that for an instant the two workers couldn't move. Then as if released by a spring both plunged into the water. When they came up out toward the middle of the pond they looked at each other a bit sheepishly.

"Mrs. Flathorns," said Paddy.

"Of course," replied Mrs. Paddy. "She must have been very near us. It was the unexpectedness of it that startled us so."

"I hope it wasn't one of those two hunters we heard calling the other night," said Paddy.

"It was Mrs. Flathorns," declared Mrs. Paddy positively. "It was her love call. Didn't you hear the loneliness in it?"

"I heard only an awful noise," said Paddy.

Just then from far away in the direction of the Great Mountain there came a faint but unmistakable grunt. Both recognized it. "Flathorns!" whispered Mrs. Paddy, and Paddy nodded.

A long silence followed. It was broken by a repetition of that

52

first frightful sound, a long-drawn, squalling bellow, startling, anything but sweet and pleasant to ears other than those for which it was intended. It seemed to come from a point on the shore where the Black Shadows had gathered closely as if they were doing their best to hide someone.

It was a few minutes before there was a reply. Then it came from far away on the side of the Great Mountain, the same deep grunt as before. This time it was a little louder for it was nearer.

A moment afterward Mrs. Flathorns stepped out in the moonlight and stood looking off in the direction from which that

grunt had seemed to come. Her big ears were set forward. She was listening.

"She knows that was Flathorns," whispered Mrs. Paddy.

"Supposing it wasn't," said Paddy.

"But of course it was," retorted Mrs. Paddy.

"I believe I will swim over and ask her," said Paddy.

"You will do nothing of the sort. You will stay right here. It is no business of ours anyway," declared Mrs. Paddy.

So Paddy did as he was bidden and side by side, close together, they floated, watching Mrs. Flathorns and wondering if she would call again. They had about decided that she wasn't going to when Mrs. Flathorns, who all the time had stood motionless, lifted her head, opened her mouth and once more that harsh, squalling bellow rang through the Green Forest. It was followed by two deep grunts. They came from different parts of the Great Mountain.

Paddy looked at Mrs. Paddy. She looked at him. "Two!" said Paddy. "What does that mean? You heard two, didn't you, my dear?"

Mrs. Paddy agreed that there had been two grunts from the mountainside. Then both looked to see what effect they had had on Mrs. Flathorns.

"She's gone!" cried Paddy.

It was so. Mrs. Flathorns was nowhere to be seen. Big as she was, and among all the Green Forest folk only Flathorns was bigger, she had made no sound in her going. It was as if she had

54

just melted into the blackness of the surrounding woods.

"She must be afraid," murmured Mrs. Paddy.

"What of?" asked Paddy. "She wouldn't be afraid of Flathorns," he added.

Then for the time being Mrs. Flathorns was forgotten. Down from the mountainside on the still air came the sound of deep grunts. They didn't sound exactly the same and they came from places some distance apart. They were angry grunts. There was no doubt whatever about that. What is more, each grunt sounded angrier, more threatening than the preceding grunts. Not only did they sound as if the grunters were moving nearer to each other, but also as if they were drawing nearer to the pond.

"They are coming this way. There is no doubt about it," declared Paddy. He sounded as if he were getting excited.

"I wonder who they are," said Mrs. Paddy uneasily.

"One of them is Flathorns. You may be sure of that," said Paddy.

"How do you know?" asked Mrs. Paddy.

"That deepest grunt is his. I would know it wherever I might hear it. Besides, what other Moose lives around here?" replied Paddy.

Mrs. Paddy shook her head. "I don't know," she confessed. "The Flathorns and their twins are the only ones I have seen. Perhaps another has just moved into the neighborhood."

"They are still coming this way. Perhaps we will have a chance to see who they are," said Paddy.

"And they are getting madder and madder about something. I wonder where Mrs. Flathorns is," whispered Mrs. Paddy.

As if in answer Mrs. Flathorns called again from where the Black Shadows had gathered most thickly. "That may be a love call but it isn't a lovely sound," whispered Paddy.

For some minutes there was silence, that stillness that could be felt. It was ended by a crash in the brush not far away and then a grunt, a deep ugly-sounding grunt. There was an answering grunt followed by the sound of a small tree being broken down and beaten to pieces. It sounded as if whoever was doing this was in a terrible rage. It was exciting and even a little frightening to the two listeners out in the water although they knew they were perfectly safe there.

"They are looking for each other," whispered Paddy.

"What for?" Mrs. Paddy wanted to know.

"To fight if those grunts mean what they sound as if they mean," replied Paddy.

"What do they want to fight for?" Mrs. Paddy asked.

"Don't ask me. Ask Mrs. Flathorns. Probably she knows," replied Paddy. But Mrs. Flathorns wasn't there to be asked.

The grunting and now and then a bellow and the thrashing about in the brush continued. Two great Moose were challenging each other, each trying to make the other think he was the bigger and stronger by making all the noise he could.

"What terrible tempers! Do you suppose they really will fight?" whispered Mrs. Paddy.

"If they are going to I hope they will come out where we can see them," replied Paddy.

Meanwhile Mrs. Flathorns was forgotten. And Paddy and Mrs. Paddy were forgetting the work that needed to be done. They floated out near their house watching and listening, too excited to think of anything but what might happen out in the moonlight on the shore of their pond.

IX. A Lady Makes Up Her Mind

Love at times may be perplexing,
Quite upsetting and most vexing.
— MRS. FLATHORNS

OF ALL THE PEOPLE in the Green Forest Mrs. Flathorns probably is the homeliest. Only Flathorns himself when without his wonderful antlers can compare with her homeliness. She has no antlers. Nothing about her appearance is pleasing. She is so big she looks awkward, but it is just looks. Big as she is she can move so quietly she has little trouble in keeping out of sight.

Spring is usually thought of as the season of love. It is with the feathered folk and some others. But with all members of the

58

Deer family autumn is the love season. Mrs. Flathorns, standing in a thicket on the shore of the little pond at the foot of the Great Mountain, listened to the angry grunting and bellowing of two Moose in the woods on the opposite shore and knew that it was because of her that they were threatening to fight. It is curious that of two things so wholly unlike as love and hate one can make the other, but so it is.

Out in the moonlight on the opposite shore stepped a great Moose. It was Flathorns. Mrs. Flathorns drew a long breath. "He is wonderful," she sighed.

Then a little way from him out stepped another great Moose. At that distance the stranger looked to be almost if not quite as big as Flathorns. Mrs. Flathorns drew another long breath. "Oh," she sighed, "he is wonderful too."

For what seemed to the three watchers a long time but was but a moment or two the two great Moose faced each other silent and motionless. Paddy held his breath. Mrs. Paddy held her breath. Over in the thicket near them Mrs. Flathorns held her breath. Suddenly as if at a signal both lowered their heads and plunged forward. The great antlers met with a clash that rang far through the Green Forest. Flathorns slipped to his knees but in a flash was up again and pushing with all his great strength. The other was pushed back a little, but only a little. They snorted and grunted. Both slipped to their knees. They parted, each backing a little. They pawed the ground, then crashed together again. This time it was Flathorns who was pushed back. They reared and struck at each other with their sharp-edged hoofs.

Mrs. Flathorns forgot that she meant to remain hidden. She moved out to the edge of the water near where Paddy and Mrs. Paddy were floating. Perhaps the two fighters saw her for now they fought with increased fury. They were fighting for her admiration and love, and their hate for each other was the hate of jealousy.

Flathorns had gloried in his great strength. He needed all of it now. The other was younger and because of this he was just a little quicker in his movements. That always is the advantage of youth. But Flathorns had the advantage of greater experience. Being older he had fought oftener. Experience always is an advantage, often one that nothing else can overcome.

Back and forth along the shore raged the fight. The ground was torn up as if by a plow. Bushes and small trees were broken and trampled down. Now one fighter, then the other, seemed to have the best of the fight. Sometimes head to head they pushed and pushed with all their strength until they were forced to rest, still head to head. Whenever one saw a chance he would rear and strike with his front feet. It was in this way that Flathorns received a cut on one shoulder.

Once the stranger slipped and by a quick thrust and twist of his antlers Flathorns upset him and struck him with hoofs and antlers before he could scramble to his feet. Neither showed any signs of giving up. Their steaming breath rose in clouds on the

60

cold night air. They grunted and snorted. Now and then one bellowed his rage.

"Aren't they wonderful?" sighed Mrs. Flathorns. "Know what?"

"What?" asked Paddy.

"I think they are fighting for me," said Mrs. Flathorns with a happy sigh.

The Green Forest had seen many fights among its people, small and great, but never a harder, more exciting fight than this one. The two great Moose, largest of all the Green Forest folk for miles around, were fighting with a fury that was truly frightful. It was an exciting fight for anyone to watch, but more exciting for Mrs. Flathorns than for anyone else because she knew, or thought she knew, that they were fighting for her.

As you know, Paddy and Mrs. Paddy were watching from the water. From the top of a tall dead tree Hooty the Great Horned Owl was looking on. Tufty the Lynx, drawn by the sound of clashing antlers, angry grunts and thudding hoofs, had crept into a thicket of young hemlock trees from which he could see without being seen. Puma was stretched along a big limb of a tree from which he could see all that went on. Old Man Coyote was looking on and so was Buster Bear.

"They are fighting for me," Mrs. Flathorns repeated over and over to herself. It was this that made that fight more exciting for her than for anyone else. It sent little thrills all over her. Which did she want to win? She didn't want either to win just yet. No, sir, she didn't. She was enjoying those exciting thrills too much to want them to end.

For a long time it was a very even fight. Sometimes Flathorns seemed to be having the best of it. Then it would be the other. Now and then one would slip to his knees as, head to head, they strained and pushed. Once both slipped down together. Kneeling, they continued to shove and tried to twist with their locked antlers to overthrow each other.

Paddy swam a little nearer to Mrs. Flathorns. "Of course you want Flathorns to win," said he.

Mrs. Flathorns didn't reply at once. You see, just then Flathorns had slipped and was being pushed back. It made the young stranger look good, very good. There was admiration in the eyes of Mrs. Flathorns as she watched him, admiration that increased with every foot that Flathorns was pushed back. Paddy repeated his question.

Mrs. Flathorns sighed. It was a gusty sort of sigh. "I want the best one to win," said she, and sighed again.

Paddy looked over at the fight. The stranger was still having a little the best of it. Paddy looked back at Mrs. Flathorns. "He is the one she really wants to win, though she didn't say so," thought he.

A few minutes later Flathorns caught the other off balance and forced him back faster than he himself had been made to back. "Isn't he wonderful?" sighed Mrs. Flathorns, and her eyes were on Flathorns with that same admiring look that but a moment before she had given the other. Paddy chuckled.

Then the stranger got his feet set and Flathorns couldn't budge him for all his splendid strength. Head to head they stood, breathing hard while they rested. When they began struggling again it was Flathorns who was pushed around. He slipped and fell. The other reared and struck with his hoofs and he struck hard.

"Isn't he wonderful?" sighed Mrs. Flathorns. Paddy chuckled again. "She doesn't know her own mind," thought he.

So the fight continued. The ground was torn and trampled. More bushes and small trees were broken down. More and more Mrs. Flathorns admired the young stranger. He was big. He was handsome if a Moose can be called handsome. And how he could fight! He wasn't a quitter. There wasn't a cowardly hair on him.

But at long last the slightly greater weight of Flathorns began to tell, and his longer experience in fighting told even more. Now it was the other who gave ground most often. Finally he was overthrown and fell heavily. When he managed to scramble to his feet he turned and ran. Flathorns plunged after him, but not far. He was too tired and out of breath. Anyway he had won.

When he returned, his great head held high in triumph, Mrs. Flathorns had made up her mind. Perhaps she had had it made up all the time. "Isn't he wonderful?" she sighed gustily. Then she gave a low whine and slipped back into the darkness. Flathorns heard it and plunged straight across the little pond. Paddy and Mrs. Paddy went back to work.

X. Locked In and Locked Out

The worker who has done his best
Will most appreciate his rest.

— PADDY THE BEAVER

FAR INTO THE NIGHT Paddy and Mrs. Paddy worked, first in getting more sticks to the food pile, then in bringing mud up from the bottom of the pond and plastering the roof of their house with it. Someone else was at work there too. It was Jack Frost. By the time the two Beavers stopped working he had covered much of the pond with thin ice.

"I think he has come to stay," said Paddy as they curled up in the comfortable room of their new house.

"Good," replied Mrs. Paddy. "We are ready for him. Now I can sleep all I want to, and I want to sleep a lot."

They slept all the next day. When in the early evening Paddy went out to the food pile and tried to put his head out of water he couldn't. He merely bumped it against ice too hard for him to break through.

He swam back to the house, taking a stick from the food pile with him. "We didn't get our new home built and ready any too soon. We are locked in," said he.

"Do you think we are locked in for the winter?" asked Mrs. Paddy drowsily.

"Yes. And everybody else is locked out," replied Paddy, eating bark from the stick he had brought in.

"Which means that there will be no enemies to watch for a long time," said Mrs. Paddy happily. "I think I will go out for a stick of food myself," she added. She slid into the water-filled hall that led out to the bottom of the pond. In a few minutes she was back with an aspen stick.

Paddy had eaten all the bark from his stick. He took it outside and presently was back with another.

"When we are ready for it I am always glad to have Jack Frost lock us in," said he. "We finished putting mud on the roof just in time. By now it is hard and Jack Frost will make it harder. Probably some visitors will come out to it on the ice, but they won't be able to tear it open. They are locked out even more completely than we are locked in for we can get exercise by swimming under the ice."

He was right when he said that probably visitors would come

66

out on the ice. Even then one was planning to do this very thing. Puma the Cougar was making his way down from the ledges not too far from the pond. He was curious about those Beavers. Not in his lifetime had there been any in that part of the Green Forest until Paddy and Mrs. Paddy had decided to build a home there. He knew nothing about their ways.

When he came in sight of the pond he saw that it was covered with ice. It was smooth and black. Nowhere was there an opening. Where were those Beavers? Were they in that house? If he could get to it he would soon find out. He was sure he could tear open the roof. Gingerly he tested the ice with a big paw and found it not yet strong enough to bear his weight.

The next morning, returning from an all-night hunt, he visited the pond. The ice was thicker and so stronger. Slowly he crept out on it until his full weight was on it. It didn't even crack. At last he could get to that house.

He was careful. Slowly he crept out until he reached the house. He circled it slowly looking for an entrance. He found none. He went around again. Then he decided to climb up on the roof. Almost at once his keen nose caught the warm tantalizing Beaver smell. It seemed to be coming up right through the top of the roof, yet he could see no opening. That smell was coming up through tiny air holes.

Inside Paddy and Mrs. Paddy could hear someone on the roof but of course they didn't know who it was. "Whoever it is he is locked out," said Paddy and refused to worry.

67

Puma sniffed and sniffed hungrily. He knew that only the thickness of the walls and roof was between him and those Beavers he had so often watched and hoped to catch. But sniffing didn't bring them any nearer and it did drive him almost crazy with desire. He dug his great claws into the sticks between which that provoking smell was coming up and tried to tear them out. The best he could do was to break off a few small bits.

That did him no good and the house no harm. Then Puma went all over that house. He scratched here. He scratched there. Wherever he scratched the result was the same. Jack Frost had done a thorough job. The mud with which that house had been plastered was so hard that even Puma's great claws were useless for breaking through it. He lost his temper. Of course that was foolish. He scratched and tore and got nowhere at all. He was dulling his claws for nothing. That house was too well built for him to start even a small hole, let alone one big enough for him to get through. If he kept on he would ruin his claws.

Inside Paddy and Mrs. Paddy listened to him and were not altogether free of anxiety. They felt sure no one could break in, but for all that they couldn't help feeling a little uneasy.

Paddy kept saying over and over, "He can't get in. He can't get in. He's locked out. I told you no one can get in and no one can."

Presently all was still outside. Had their unwelcome visitor left? They wished they knew. But they couldn't know for there was no way for them to look outside. As a matter of fact Puma was still there. He was crouched near the top, unwilling to admit that he was beaten, yet forced to admit it. All the time that tantalizing smell was making him hungrier and hungrier.

He knew he was foolish to stay there, but somehow he couldn't tear himself away. So he continued to crouch there, motionless save for the twitching tip of his long tail. He was tormented by the smell of a dinner he couldn't get, a dinner so

69

very near yet beyond his reach. Had you been where you could watch the tip of that tail you would have guessed that inside he was growing angrier and angrier.

At last, no longer hearing anyone on the roof, Paddy made up his mind that no one was there. "That fellow, whoever he was, has gone," he declared. "I'm hungry and I am going out to the food pile for something to eat."

He slipped into the underwater passage leading outside on the bottom of the pond and swam straight for the big pile of food sticks under the ice. He would pull out a stick, take it back in the house, and strip off the bark he liked so much.

Now it happened that just as Paddy left the house on his way to the food pile Puma looked down from his place on the roof. The new ice covering the pond was as clear as window glass. It was so clear that it didn't seem as if there were any ice there.

So when Puma looked down on Paddy, who upon leaving the house had come up just under the ice, it seemed to Puma that he could reach out a paw and touch him. Yes, sir, that is the way it seemed.

With the smell of Beaver still tantalizing him, and with Paddy himself right under his eyes, Puma forgot where he was. He forgot the ice which he was looking through without seeing it. He thought of nothing but the fact that at long last Paddy the Beaver was within easy jumping distance and no one to interfere. He must act quickly for that Beaver was swimming away. He did. He gathered his powerful hind legs under him for one of his mighty leaps. Paddy was moving away. In a moment he would be beyond reach. Puma leaped.

Crash! Smash! Splash! Puma had landed on the ice and broken through into the cold water! The ice had been strong enough for him to walk on but not strong enough to hold his heavy weight when he sprang down on it from the top of the house.

Br-r-r-r-r, how cold that water was! Like most members of the Cat family Puma wasn't fond of the water anyway. Being plunged into it when it was ice cold chilled his hot blood, and his hot temper as well.

As Puma broke through Paddy dodged to one side, then turned back and swam as fast as he could for the house. He didn't stop to see what might happen to Puma. He was as badly frightened as was Puma, and Puma really was frightened. He kicked and struggled and splashed. The ice broke when he tried to climb out on it. When at last he did get out he was a sorry-looking person. As he sneaked away he shivered and shook. For the time being he had lost all interest in a Beaver dinner. And it was all because he had not really looked before he leaped.

XI. Each to His Own Way

Beware the ones who boldly say
That theirs is the appointed way.
— OLD MOTHER NATURE

OLD MAN COYOTE stood on the shore of Paddy's pond. He looked out across the still black surface to where the roof of the Beaver house stood high above the ice. It was clear black ice. Of course it wasn't really black. It was the water under it that made it look so. For several minutes Old Man Coyote stood looking at the house. Then he sighed. "I would so like a Beaver dinner, but they are locked in and I am locked out," said he.

He started to trot across the ice to the dam, then changed his mind and went over to the house. He approached it cautiously. There was no reason for this. It was habit. Old Man Coyote is a cautious person. He walked around the house until he was just above the underwater doorway. He didn't know this until he happened to look down and saw a big brown form come out from the house. It was Paddy.

Old Man Coyote's mouth watered. He couldn't help it. Here was a wonderful dinner with only a not-very-thick sheet of ice and a little water between it and him. Yet it might just as well have been on the moon. It would have been no more impossible to get.

Paddy swam beneath the ice and Old Man Coyote walked along on it just above him. Perhaps Paddy saw Old Man Coyote, but it is doubtful. However, the latter saw Paddy clearly. He was curious to see where Paddy was going. It didn't take long to find out. Paddy swam straight to his food pile. Old Man Coyote watched him tug and pull at a stick until he got it free, then followed him back to the house.

Old Man Coyote scratched at the wall of the house. It was hard, too hard to be torn open. There wasn't a chance. Perhaps there might be a place on top that wasn't so well protected with frozen mud. He jumped up, then wished he hadn't. Can you guess why? It was for the very same reason that Puma had wished that he hadn't climbed up there. Coming up through tiny air holes was that tantalizing Beaver smell and Old Man Coyote was very, very hungry. For a moment he scratched frantically with both paws, but it was only for a moment. It was perfectly useless and he knew it. He grinned at his own foolishness, jumped down and went on his way. It was long since he had had a really good meal. It seemed to him that these days he was hungry all the time. Cold weather had brought hard times to many. Old Man Coyote was one of them.

In the big comfortable room which was both bedroom and living room Paddy and Mrs. Paddy spent most of their time sleeping. They were making up for the sleep lost while they were working so hard to get ready for winter. When they were hungry they brought a food stick into the house and ate all the bark from it. Then the bare stick was taken outside. Sometimes it was used to strengthen the house. Sometimes it was left where it could be picked up later if there should be need for it. Now and then a stick was taken over to the dam.

While Old Man Coyote, Puma, and others were hungry much of the time, and spending most of their time roaming far and wide hunting for something to eat, Paddy and Mrs. Paddy were enjoying the peace and rest which they had so well earned by courage and hard work. Now there was no work to be done. There was nothing to worry about. Under the ice enough food was stored to last them until spring and warm weather. It made not the smallest difference what the weather outside might be. Brother North Wind might howl and shriek and pile the snow deep; they wouldn't even know it. Jack Frost might do his worst until the trees cracked with the cold, but he couldn't touch them. Beneath the ice the water was always the same. Their thick waterproof fur coats kept them thoroughly warm at all times. Not for anything in all the Great World would they have changed places with any of the other Green Forest folk. Peace and contentment were theirs. Best of all they had earned it.

But with Old Man Coyote life was very, very different. Hunting was very poor and getting worse. Anyway, it seemed so to him. For several days he hadn't found enough for a full meal. It seemed as if even the Mice had gone away. Anyway, they had gone into hiding everywhere he hunted, or else someone had been ahead of him and caught them. A Mouse was only a bite, and often it was a long time between bites.

When he had looked down through the ice and seen Paddy just under him he had felt much as you would feel if you were very, very hungry and stood outside a window looking in with only a pane of glass between you and a wonderful dinner all ready to eat. And then there had been the tantalizing smell of the dinner he couldn't get. He told Mrs. Coyote about it.

"I should have known better than to go over there," said he. "I went just to do a little hunting around that pond. I knew Jack Frost had been around, but I forgot that he turns water so hard. I could walk on it right out to that house and I did. That was another foolish thing to do for I knew beforehand that I couldn't possibly get into it. And then I saw one of those Beavers right under me and I couldn't touch him. That was too much. It really was, my dear. Then to see him take his food into the house and know that he was sitting there inside eating his fill while I was so hungry I could have eaten bare bones!"

75

Mrs. Coyote looked thoughtful. "Those Beavers have it soft and easy, don't they?" said she.

"I'll say they do," agreed Old Man Coyote. "They never have to worry about where the next meal is coming from. All they have to do is swim just a little way and get it, and they can do this whenever they feel hungry. They don't even have to look for it. It is right there waiting for them. All they do is eat and sleep. They don't care a slap of their tails what the weather is. Rain or snow, sunshine or clouds, bitter cold or warm days, it is all the same to them. They don't really know what winter is. Sometimes I wonder if they know how lucky they are."

"Are they lucky?" asked Mrs. Coyote.

"What do you think?" retorted Old Man Coyote.

"I just wonder," replied Mrs. Coyote mildly.

Old Man Coyote looked at her sharply. "My dear," said he, "wouldn't you think yourself lucky if you could spend a whole winter in perfect comfort, doing nothing but eat and sleep? Wouldn't you?"

"And never go anywhere?" said Mrs. Coyote.

Old Man Coyote scratched his nose. "I hadn't thought of that," said he.

"And never see anyone or anything?" said Mrs. Coyote.

"That's so! They don't, do they? They really are prisoners. I hadn't thought of that either," replied Old Man Coyote.

"Do you remember the work they did last fall?" asked Mrs. Coyote.

"Now you speak of it I do," he replied.

"Would you like to work like that?" asked Mrs. Coyote.

Old Man Coyote grinned. "What do you think?" he asked in his turn.

"I've tried bark, but I've never found any that seemed to me like food," said Mrs. Coyote.

"And that is all they have to eat all winter long," said Old Man Coyote thoughtfully.

"That is what I have been told," replied Mrs. Coyote.

"I wouldn't like that. I wouldn't like that at all. Know what?" said Old Man Coyote.

"What?" asked Mrs. Coyote.

"It is we who are lucky, not those Beavers," replied Old Man Coyote.

"Lucky in what way?" Mrs. Coyote wanted to know.

"In not having to live the way they do — locked in, nothing to do, nowhere to go, nothing to see, and only bark to eat. My dear, we are lucky even if we are hungry. Come on, let's go look for Mice!" Old Man Coyote grinned. Mrs. Coyote grinned back at him. Then they separated to hunt for a dinner.

XII. The Whispering Water

When once a task is well begun
The doing of it should be fun.
— PADDY THE BEAVER

WORK wherein there is no pleasure is work indeed. Nowhere among the Green Forest folk will you find harder workers than the Beavers. Yet nowhere will you find folk who get more pleasure and happiness out of living.

Almost all winter Paddy and Mrs. Paddy had had nothing to do but eat and sleep. Until now they had enjoyed this for they had worked hard all through the fall. But enough is enough no matter how good it is, and they had had enough. They began to look ahead to the coming of spring.

"We must look over the dam for leaks before high water comes," said Paddy.

"Of course," replied Mrs. Paddy. "A little work now may save much work later. I am glad there is something we can do now. It will be fun."

So they made many trips under the ice to the dam. Of course from under the ice they could look the dam over from only one side. To climb out and look the dam over thoroughly they would have to wait until there was open water. They added a stick here, a little mud there.

"It is good to work again," said Paddy.

"Your mistake," said Mrs. Paddy.

"How so?" asked Paddy.

"This isn't work; it is fun," replied Mrs. Paddy. "We are not doing much, but it is better than doing nothing. Sometimes I think that we Beavers are the only folks in the Green Forest who really know how to live."

Paddy chuckled. "Probably other folks think the same about themselves and pity us," said he.

"Pity!" exclaimed Mrs. Paddy. "Why in the world should anybody pity us?"

"For having to work," replied Paddy. There was a twinkle in his eyes. Mrs. Paddy didn't see it.

"Pity us for having to work?" she cried. "Why, folks who don't work don't really live. They don't know how to. The way to enjoy doing nothing is first to work for it. Doing things is fun."

"So you think work is fun," said Paddy.

"Well, perhaps hard work isn't really fun, but there is pleasure in it if you look for it. The trouble with some people is that they don't look for it. In a way I'm sorry for those folks. You can't get the most from a good time without having earned it by working for it." It was clear that Mrs. Paddy meant what she said.

"Just the same, I am glad there is no big hole in the dam that must be filled quickly," declared Paddy. "Work is wonderful when it isn't the wrong kind or there isn't too much of it."

"I believe you are getting lazy," declared Mrs. Paddy.

A few days later when Paddy returned to the house with a food stick, he said that the weather must be getting warmer.

"What makes you think so?" asked Mrs. Paddy.

"The water is beginning to whisper," replied Paddy, chewing a piece of bark.

"Don't talk with your mouth full," chided Mrs. Paddy. "I presume you mean that the water is moving through the pond a little faster."

Paddy nodded. He was still chewing a mouthful of bark. Mrs. Paddy waited until he pulled off another piece of bark. Then she asked, "Does that mean anything in particular?"

"It means," mumbled Paddy, "that ice and snow are beginning to melt and so more water is going through."

"I wish you wouldn't talk with your mouth full. Are you sure of it?" said Mrs. Paddy.

"Sure of what?" Paddy turned the stick in his hands so that he could gnaw off more bark.

"That the water has really begun to whisper?" replied Mrs. Paddy.

Paddy merely nodded and went right on gnawing bark from that stick. It was nearly bare by this time.

"I am going out to see for myself," declared Mrs. Paddy. She yawned, then slipped into the water-filled passage that led outside. When she returned she brought an aspen stick to nibble on.

"Well, my dear, was the water whispering?" asked Paddy when she had her mouth full of bark.

Mrs. Paddy nodded. "It was *talking*," she mumbled.

"Speaking of talking, I wish you wouldn't do it with your mouth full," said Paddy, and disappeared with the bare stick, taking it outside.

When he returned Mrs. Paddy wanted to know if the water was still talking. "Still talking, and it is getting to be more than a whisper," replied Paddy.

"I wonder if it is saying the same thing it was when I was out for this stick," said Mrs. Paddy.

"What was it saying then?" asked Paddy.

" 'Look ahead. Look ahead,' " replied Mrs. Paddy. With her great orange-colored cutting teeth she began shredding her stick to bits to add to her bed of shredded wood.

Paddy chuckled. "That is what it always says when it is talking — 'Look ahead. Look ahead,' " said he.

"There is no need for it to tell us that. It is what we have done all our lives," said Mrs. Paddy.

"True, my dear. Quite true," replied Paddy. "We were looking ahead when we built the dam that makes our pond, and when we built this house and made the entrance where the water is too deep for Jack Frost to close it with ice. And again when we cut and stored in the pond enough food to last us all winter. Between you and me I don't see how some folks who never look ahead manage to live. I really don't."

Mrs. Paddy finished shredding her stick and arranging her bed. "Did that talking water tell you we will have an early spring?" she asked.

Paddy pulled off a piece of aspen bark and ate it before he answered. "What does running water know of what is going to be?" said he. "All it knows is what *is*. Comes a little warm weather and ice and snow begin to melt and water runs. That doesn't mean an early spring. Jack Frost comes back. Snow and ice stop melting and water stops running. All that talking water outside says is 'Look ahead! Look ahead!'" Paddy looked at Mrs. Paddy and grinned.

"Just so," she agreed. "Whether spring comes early or spring comes late there are certain things that must be done, and that talking water is reminding us of this. For one I am glad to be reminded. Until lately we have done hardly a thing but sleep and eat since the pond was frozen over. Know what?"

Paddy shook his head. "What?" he asked.

"I'm very very tired — of doing nothing," replied Mrs. Paddy.

"You mean you are so rested that you are tired of resting," said Paddy. "I feel the same way. Whether Mistress Spring will arrive early or late we don't know. It doesn't matter. It doesn't matter at all. What we do know is that she will surely come, and when she does we must be ready for her. If she comes early a lot of water will come rushing down into our pond all at once, a flood. If she is late the ice and snow will melt more slowly and there will not be so much water rushing through the pond at one time. Whether she comes early or late, it makes no real difference to us. We must — "

"Look ahead," interrupted Mrs. Paddy mischievously.

"Just so. You said it, my dear," retorted Paddy. "We don't know what will happen, but we must hope for the best and make ready for the worst."

Outside the water coming down Laughing Brook from the Great Mountain was ever so lazily moving in a gentle current through the middle of the pond. You know it was the dam across Laughing Brook that made the pond. It was that gentle current that was talking. It still was saying, "Look ahead. Look ahead."

XIII. Trouble Begins

No mighty tree, however tall,
But started very, very small.
— OLD MOTHER NATURE

PADDY WAS WORRIED. He had brought in a food stick, but instead of sitting down to eat the bark from it he laid it down and turned to go out again.

"Where are you going?" Mrs. Paddy wanted to know.

"To look for trouble," replied Paddy.

"Usually trouble comes without being looked for. What is worrying you now?" asked Mrs. Paddy.

"There is more air space under the ice than there has been," Paddy replied.

Mrs. Paddy looked disturbed. "That means water is running out of the pond faster than it is running in, and that means — "

"A leak in the dam," Paddy finished for her.

He didn't need to suggest that she go with him. Outside she found at once why Paddy was worried. All winter there had been almost no space at all between the water and the ice. Now there was space. She followed Paddy over to the dam.

A bad break in their dam is about the worst thing that can happen to Beavers. It is the one thing they fear most. An empty pond, or one with very little water in it, means constant danger from hungry enemies. So the Beaver folk keep careful watch of the water. As soon as they discover that there is less than there should be they go looking for a leak. They don't put it off. It is something to be done at once.

Still under the ice Mrs. Paddy went one way along the dam and Paddy went the other way. Presently he found a place where there was a small leak. There was no hole to be seen but the water was working through the dam. There was just a very little current there. Probably you or I wouldn't have noticed it.

Paddy went to work at once. From the bottom of the pond he brought up mud and plastered it between the sticks of the dam at that place. Mrs. Paddy joined him and soon the water stopped running through the dam. After a bit the water began to rise very slowly in the pond.

"It was only a little hole," said Mrs. Paddy when they were back in the house.

"I am afraid of little holes," replied Paddy. "I am going to watch the place where this one was. I hope it will stay fixed."

"I don't know why it shouldn't. It wasn't enough of a hole to be seen," said Mrs. Paddy.

"Not on our side," replied Paddy. "There are two sides."

"Of course. What of it?" demanded Mrs. Paddy.

"We didn't see the other side, the outer side," replied Paddy.

"I hadn't thought of that!" exclaimed Mrs. Paddy. "I know what you are thinking — that on the other side the hole may be bigger. Is that it?"

Paddy nodded. "A small hole on one side could become a big hole on the other side. I would feel a lot better had I been able

to look at the other side. If only there was a hole in the ice through which we could climb out on the dam we could find out just how things are," he explained.

"We stopped the leak, so why worry?" said Mrs. Paddy.

"I'm not really worrying, just a little uneasy. That was only a patch job and it will need watching. We could use nothing but mud and that could be washed away, especially if there is a big hole on the other side," replied Paddy.

A while later he went out to get a food stick. He was gone so long Mrs. Paddy went to look for him. She found him working at the place where the leak had been.

"Some of the mud had washed out and the water was beginning to leak through again," he explained.

Mrs. Paddy helped and once more the leak was stopped. Back in the house they lay down for a nap. It wasn't a long nap. When they awoke Paddy slipped out to make sure that all was well. Mrs. Paddy followed. She was becoming uneasy, too. Again they found the leak had opened a little. It was soon fixed and they swam back to the house.

"Now I *am* worried," admitted Paddy. "I fear there is a big hole on the other side and that is why the mud washes through. It makes a weak place in the dam. If a lot of water should come rushing down the dam might break right there. Then where would we be?"

"In trouble," replied Mrs. Paddy.

"You said it!" cried Paddy.

As long as ice covered all the pond they were prisoners in a way, prisoners in their own home. They kept patching that leak on the inside of the dam and wishing they could get at the other side. At first it was not too bad. But when Sister South Wind began melting the snow, and the water came down Laughing Brook faster and faster, the mud washed out almost as fast as they could put it in.

At long last the ice melted enough for them to climb out on the dam. They found what they had feared to find, a big hole on the other side. By now water was coming through fast. When Paddy tried to place sticks in that hole they were washed away and carried off down Laughing Brook, now free of ice and bank-full of rushing water.

Two badly worried Beavers felt very helpless. "If," said Paddy, "we could only have worked at this when the trouble began."

"*If* is the most useless word I know," grumbled Mrs. Paddy, tugging a stick toward the hole.

"Why useless?" asked Paddy, as a stick he was trying to put in place was washed away.

"Because whatever it refers to has already happened, or will happen, or can't happen, or won't happen, and nothing can be done about it. So what good is it?" retorted Mrs. Paddy.

Before Paddy could reply the thing they feared, and were working so hard to prevent, happened. Pressing hard against the weak place the water broke through with a rush, tearing out sticks and other stuff of which the dam was built. It was lucky for the two workers that neither happened to be in the way at the time. Sadly they climbed up on the dam and watched the break grow bigger and bigger and the water in the pond become lower and lower. Just then there was nothing they could do about it.

It was some time before either of them spoke. Then Paddy said, "I can't sit around doing nothing."

"What can we do? We can't work in that water. It is too swift," said Mrs. Paddy.

"After a while it won't be so swift," said Paddy.

"And by that time our pond will be only a puddle," moaned Mrs. Paddy.

"We don't have to wait for that. We can go to work now, cutting small trees and brush ready to use when we can work on that break," said Paddy.

"What are we waiting for?" cried Mrs. Paddy. She started down from the dam.

Slap! That was Paddy's broad tail brought down on the top of the dam. Mrs. Paddy stopped, looking this way and that way for danger.

"There isn't any," said Paddy mildly. "Not just now anyway. But there may be later. There surely will be. So it won't do for both of us to be down there at work away from the water."

"What danger?" Mrs. Paddy wanted to know.

"How long do you think it will be before news of this break will get around in the Green Forest? Not very long. And when it does we will have visitors. Supposing Tufty the Lynx should find both of us down there at work," said Paddy.

"I don't want to think of it," declared Mrs. Paddy.

"Or Puma the Cougar, or Old Man Coyote, or Buster Bear," continued Paddy.

Mrs. Paddy shivered a little, although the air wasn't cold enough to be felt through that wonderful, waterproof, thick fur coat of hers. "What shall we do?" she asked.

"One of us will work down there while the other stays up here watching. We'll take turn and turn about," explained Paddy.

Mrs. Paddy agreed, so this was what they did. Long ago they had learned that there were times when it wasn't safe for both to be working and no one watching. And they had learned, too, that whatever happens in the Green Forest soon is known by all who live there. Paddy had no doubt at all that news of the broken dam was already spreading fast and they would not be allowed to work in peace very long. It wasn't as long as he hoped.

XIV. Paddy's Close Call

Though danger may appear in work
It gives you no excuse to shirk.

— PADDY THE BEAVER

IT WAS PADDY'S TURN to cut brush and young trees while Mrs. Paddy kept watch. He had started to get down from the dam when Mrs. Paddy stopped him. "What is it? Did you see someone?" he asked.

"I don't know," confessed Mrs. Paddy. "I thought something moved at the edge of the roots of that fallen tree, but I'm not sure. Sometimes I wish we Beavers had better eyes."

Sitting close together they watched for a few minutes. Nothing moved over by those upturned roots. Paddy became impatient. "Keep your eyes open and if you see danger just whack a signal with your tail," said he and went down to work. Mrs. Paddy continued to watch that fallen tree with the upturned roots. She was still suspicious. She wished she could see back of them. If she could have she would have seen Old Man Coyote crouching there, peeping through a small opening between two roots. Now and then he licked his lips hungrily.

Whisky Jack the Canada Jay, own cousin to Sammy Jay of the blue coat, came flitting from tree to tree. He saw Paddy at work and he saw the water rushing through the break in the dam. "So that is the news Old Man Coyote meant," he chuckled.

Paddy looked up suspiciously. "Where is Old Man Coyote?" he demanded.

"How should I know?" retorted Whisky Jack. "I saw him a while ago but it was a long way from here down Laughing Brook. He said Laughing Brook had brought him some news, but he wouldn't say what it was. Smart rascal, Old Man Coyote."

Paddy made no reply. He quit work and joined Mrs. Paddy on the dam. "I wonder if you did see something move over by the roots of that old tree," said he.

"I guess not. Nothing has moved over there since," she replied.

Meanwhile Old Man Coyote was wishing he could make himself as small as a Mouse. He had flattened himself on the ground back of those roots. He didn't so much as twitch an ear. Through a peephole between the roots he could see the Beavers on their dam and Whisky Jack. He watched the latter closely.

"As long as that fellow is around I will have no chance for a Beaver dinner," thought he. "His eyes are too bright. As long as he is around it won't do for me to so much as wink an eye." So when finally Whisky Jack flew off without discovering him he drew a long breath.

It soon was plain to him that Paddy and Mrs. Paddy were uneasy. They were suspicious and seemed to be growing more so. They seemed to have decided to stop work. He wondered why. He was sure that neither of them had seen him. He wished he were near enough to overhear what they were talking about.

"Whisky Jack thinks that Old Man Coyote knows about this break in the dam; that Laughing Brook told him. If that is so he will be around soon," Paddy was saying.

"If he isn't around already, which he probably is," said Mrs. Paddy. She looked over at the fallen tree. She was still suspicious.

"I have an unpleasant feeling," said Paddy.

"What feeling?" asked Mrs. Paddy.

"That we are being watched this very minute," said Paddy.

"I have had that feeling for some time," replied Mrs. Paddy.

"Being watched usually means danger ahead, but there is nothing we can do about it now. So let's go get something to eat; I'm hungry," declared Paddy.

They slipped into the water. As they swam to their food pile they realized what a lot of water had already run out from the pond through that break. It must be mended just as soon as the rush of water through it lessened enough to allow them to work there.

The moment they left the dam Old Man Coyote, first making sure that Whisky Jack was nowhere around, moved nearer where those Beavers had been at work. He hid behind a boulder. He was sure that there he was near enough to catch one before it would be possible to scramble over the dam into deep water. He was nicely hidden by the time Paddy and Mrs. Paddy returned to the dam. He licked his lips as he waited and watched.

They climbed out on the dam at the edge of the break and looked at the water rushing through. It wasn't as swift as it had been. "I believe I can work down in there now. Anyway, I am going to try," said Paddy.

They looked all around. They saw nothing and heard nothing to arouse suspicion. Long ago they had learned that where there is a chance for danger there danger is almost sure to be lurking. "I still have that feeling of being watched," said Mrs. Paddy as Paddy started down off the dam.

"I have it too," said he. "But there is work to do and it can't wait."

He climbed down from the dam and headed for the little pile of sticks already cut. Behind the big boulder Old Man Coyote made ready to move quickly. He would wait until Paddy was as near as he was likely to come, then spring out and rush for him. He was sure he could catch Paddy before he could climb up on the dam and dive into the water on the other side. He was very sure of that Beaver dinner now.

On the dam Mrs. Paddy grew more and more uneasy. She couldn't get rid of that feeling of being watched. It was so strong that she was extra watchful if that were possible. So it was that when Old Man Coyote changed his position ever so little to watch Paddy she saw the slight movement. Someone was behind that big boulder! She didn't wait to find out who it was. She lifted her broad tail and brought it down with a startling, loud whack.

It was as if when it struck that tail released a spring that set Paddy's legs going. He dropped a stick he had just picked up. He didn't look to see what the danger was. Long ago he had learned that safety first is the basic rule for long life, and until this has been heeded nothing else matters. What a pity so many boys and girls, older folk too, have not learned this most important rule, or are heedless of it. It is very sad.

Quick as Paddy was in starting Old Man Coyote was as quick. He leaped from behind that boulder and was after Paddy with twice Paddy's speed. Paddy is stout, heavy, and has short legs. He is not built for fast running.

He was doing his best, but he wouldn't be able to reach the dam in time. In another minute Old Man Coyote would be on him. Looking on from the dam Mrs. Paddy closed her eyes for just a moment. In that moment Paddy had turned sharply to one side so suddenly that Old Man Coyote had missed his jump. She opened them just in time to see Paddy plunge into the water rushing down Laughing Brook through the break in the dam. Would he be able to swim against it?

It was not at all what Old Man Coyote had expected. He wasn't prepared for that sudden turn. He stood on the bank watching the dinner he had been so sure of so near yet out of reach, for he was not at home in the water as Paddy was. He still hoped a little for he is not one to give up easily. Perhaps that swift water would sweep Paddy back within his reach. He followed along on the bank. It was a very little way to the break in the dam where the water was rushing through with such force he doubted if anybody could swim against it.

"I'll get him there if I don't before," thought Old Man Coyote.

He was making the mistake that so many people make, of judging others by themselves. Self is a poor standard by which to judge another. It makes no allowance for differences. Old Man Coyote wasn't built for swimming, just as Paddy wasn't built for running. One was at home on land and the other in water. Paddy was proving what a splendid swimmer he is. Slowly but steadily he moved ahead. Of all the other Green Forest folk only Little Joe Otter could have moved upstream in that rushing water.

From the top of the dam Mrs. Paddy watched. Never had she been more anxious. Would Paddy be able to make it? She knew that the day before he couldn't have. But by now so much water had run out of the pond that the current wasn't so strong. While she watched Paddy she also watched Old Man Coyote. She was ready to dive into the pond should he try to catch her.

The few minutes following Paddy's plunge into Laughing Brook were exciting for all three. Old Man Coyote was excited, torn between disappointment and hope. Mrs. Paddy was excited, watching and also hoping. Paddy was excited, wondering if he would have enough strength to get through into the pond.

Old Man Coyote crouched at the very edge of the water close to the dam. Slowly, very slowly, Paddy swam in the rushing water almost under his very nose and there was nothing he could do about it. Out in the pond Mrs. Paddy now waited anxiously. For just a moment she was afraid Paddy wouldn't make it. Then he was through and swimming easily in the comparatively quiet water of the pond. She swam to meet him. Old Man Coyote jumped up on the dam and watched them touch noses.

"Good dinners for some other time," said he and grinned. Long ago he learned to grin at disappointment. It helps.

XV. Just in Time

If you will to yourself be true
Let nothing stop what you should do.
— PADDY THE BEAVER

A JOB TO BE DONE is an obligation no self-respecting Beaver ever thinks of trying to avoid. There was a job to be done now, a job that couldn't wait. By and by wouldn't do. It wouldn't do at all. There was a break in the dam and the water was rushing through. Unless the dam was fixed at once the water in the pond would soon be so low that Paddy and Mrs. Paddy wouldn't be safe there, not even in their own house.

They knew this. So did Old Man Coyote. So did Tufty the Lynx. So did Buster Bear, who had awakened from his winter

99

sleep a few days before. Old Man Coyote was the first one there and as you know he almost caught Paddy. Shortly afterward Buster Bear came shuffling along. He stopped to look at the hole in the dam. Then he stood up on his hind legs to look over into the pond. The water was getting low.

"I'll stay around a while," thought Buster. "If that dam isn't mended all the water will run out, or enough of it for me to get out to that house and tear it open." Then he turned and showed his teeth to Tufty the Lynx who had come sneaking out from under some low boughs. He also wanted a look at the break in the dam.

Meanwhile Paddy and Mrs. Paddy were planning what to do. "That dam must be fixed right away," declared Paddy.

"It certainly must," agreed Mrs. Paddy. "But how are we to do it? We may be sure Old Man Coyote is somewhere around. It won't be safe to try again for those sticks where he so nearly caught you, and we must have sticks."

"You are right, my dear. It won't be safe to try for those sticks. In fact, it won't be safe to go ashore at all. So — " Paddy paused.

"So what?" asked Mrs. Paddy impatiently.

"So we won't," replied Paddy.

"If we don't go ashore how can we mend the dam? How can we get the sticks?" Mrs. Paddy wanted to know. She looked puzzled. She was.

"There are enough sticks in the pond right now, mostly on

the bottom, food sticks from which we ate the bark in the winter. With these we can mend the dam without going on land at all. We'll fill that hole from the water on this side. Come on! We'll fool Old Man Coyote and Buster Bear and Tufty the Lynx," cried Paddy.

Mrs. Paddy looked surprised. "How do you know Buster Bear and Tufty are around?" she asked.

Paddy grinned. "I don't," said he. "But it is a safe guess that they are. Now let's get busy. We have a job to do."

On the other side of the dam Old Man Coyote and Tufty were quarreling. "Those Beavers are mine. I was here first," growled Old Man Coyote. He drew back his lips to show his long sharp teeth.

"They are not yours and won't be until you catch them," snarled Tufty. He showed his own teeth and they were no more pleasant to look at than were Old Man Coyote's.

Buster Bear shuffled over to tell them that both were wrong. "They are mine. Now get out, both of you," he growled in his deepest, most rumbly, grumbly voice.

Such unpleasantness as followed! The foolish three were so busy quarreling over a dinner none had that they forgot everything else. They forgot those Beavers had ears and could hear them. Meanwhile the latter were working hard. They knew opportunity when they saw it, and were making the most of it.

They brought up old food sticks from the bottom of the pond and with them were filling the hole. Some of the time they worked under water. At no time were more than heads and shoulders out of water as they worked sticks into place. Now and then a stick would be swept away, but this didn't discourage them. They brought up mud from the bottom and masses of water-soaked leaves which they packed in between the sticks. They chuckled and worked a little faster as they heard the growling and snarling of the foolish three, not one of whom discovered what was going on while they quarreled.

"Silly things," said Paddy. "If they had kept their tongues still we might not have known they were about."

"Quarreling always is silly. Do you suppose we can finish this job without too much danger?" replied Mrs. Paddy.

"Of course we can," declared Paddy. "I hope they will keep right on quarreling. They don't know yet that we are at work."

Buster Bear was the first to find it out. He looked over the top of the dam and it seemed to him that there was more water in the pond than when he had last looked. He paid no more attention to the others. He went over for a close look at the break. A stick was pushed into place from the other side. He stood up and looked over just in time to see Paddy dive, slapping the water with his tail as he went under. This was a warning to Mrs. Paddy and to let Buster know he had been seen.

Buster tried to tear the hole larger but the best he could do was to pull out a very few sticks, and these were replaced with others as fast as he pulled them out. "Woof!" snorted Buster in disgust and shuffled away.

After a while Old Man Coyote and Tufty saw that they were simply wasting time by hanging around there. So the busy workers were left in peace. However, they were just as watchful as if they knew those hungry hunters were still there.

At last the work was done. The break in the dam was filled and it was as tight and strong there as in any other part. It was finished none too soon for the weather was warm and up on the Great Mountain snow was melting fast. More and more water was rushing down Laughing Brook. The pond filled fast. By the time the last sticks were in place the water was beginning to run over the dam in several places.

"We got it done just in time," said Paddy.

"Just in time is time enough," said Mrs. Paddy. So it was. It always is. But of course it is better to be in time without the "just." Don't you think so?

They swam over to the house. Mrs. Paddy climbed out on the roof. Paddy floated close by. They were resting, for they were tired. By and by Mrs. Paddy dived and went into the house. When she returned she looked worried. "Do you know what will happen if the water gets much higher?" she asked.

"What?" replied Paddy. He knew but he asked just the same.

"It will be over the floor and our beds. It is almost there now," replied Mrs. Paddy, looking more anxious than ever.

"That would be too bad, but worse can happen," said Paddy. The anxious look was on his face now.

"What?" Mrs. Paddy looked startled.

"The dam could break again and the whole thing be washed away," replied Paddy.

Mrs. Paddy forgot about the house. She looked over to the dam. In several places the water was running over the top. "Do you know what I think?" she demanded.

"What do you think?" Paddy wanted to know.

"I think we should be over there this very minute looking for little leaks," said Mrs. Paddy.

"The very thing I was about to say," replied Paddy. "Little leaks can soon become big leaks, and the whole dam washed out. As long as there is so much water we must keep watch of the dam from end to end, stopping little leaks. Come on, my dear."

Here and there along the top of the dam were places a little lower than the rest. At these places the water poured over in little waterfalls. No attention was paid to these. They were what might be called spillways, letting the water spill out of the too full pond. That was a very good thing. If it spilled fast enough it would not get too high back there in the house.

They looked the dam over carefully from end to end. When they found a place where water trickled through faster than they thought it should they stopped it. In a couple of places the water was working through under the dam. This was bad. They dived and plugged these places from the pond side. Now and then they rested, floating in the pond or sitting on the dam, but never for long at a time. No little leaks would become big leaks if they could help it.

XVI. The Voice of Spring

The sweetness of a sound you'll find
Not in the ear but in the mind.

— PADDY THE BEAVER

IT WAS almost shadowtime of a pleasant day that had been quite warm. "Hark!" cried Paddy.

Mrs. Paddy listened. She heard nothing but the sound of rushing water coming down Laughing Brook into the pond, and the splash of it spilling over the dam. "Well," said she after a moment, "what is it I am supposed to listen for?"

"Hark!" repeated Paddy.

This time she heard it. The sound was faint, coming from far away, but there was no mistaking it. No, sir, there was no mistaking that sound — "*Honk, k'honk, onk, onk, onk, k'honk, onk, onk.*" There is no other sound like it.

Mrs. Paddy drew a long breath. "I hear it," said she. "Do you know of any sweeter sound than the voice of Spring?"

Paddy chuckled. "I wonder what Mistress Spring would say if she heard you call that her voice," said he.

"Well, if it isn't really her voice it is sweet enough to be. She would know what I mean," retorted Mrs. Paddy. She was still listening. The sound was louder and clearer now — "*Honk, k'honk, onk, onk, onk, onk, honk, onk, onk.*"

Once more Paddy chuckled. "Did you say sweet?" he asked.

"I said sweet. You may know of a sweeter sound but I don't," retorted Mrs. Paddy a little sharply. She didn't like being laughed at.

Paddy stopped chuckling. "Right, my dear. You are quite right," said he. "Judging by what it means rather than just by ear it is about the sweetest sound we can wish to hear at this time of year. When we hear good old Honker the Goose and his flock we know that Mistress Spring is with them, or close behind. I wonder if they will stop here tonight."

"I hope they will," said Mrs. Paddy. A moment later she added, "They are beginning to come down now."

"Do you see them? I can't," said Paddy.

"No. There are trees in the way. But I can hear them," replied Mrs. Paddy.

107

Once more Paddy chuckled. "I hope so," said he. "If you couldn't there would be something wrong, very wrong, with your hearing. Gracious, what a racket!"

"They are tired. They must have flown a long way today. They are very, very tired. I can tell by their voices. I guess they will be glad to get here," declared Mrs. Paddy, paying no attention to Paddy's remark.

"You seem to know a lot about them without having even seen them yet," said Paddy. He was teasing her.

She took no notice of this. "They will be here in a minute or two," said she. . . . "There they are now!"

Sure enough, out of the growing dusk appeared a flock of big birds black against the faint glow in the early evening sky. That they saw the little pond the excitement in their voices permitted no doubt. The honking became a gabbling as they circled above the pond once, twice and then a third time.

"There is good old Honker in the lead! He is taking no chances even though he must see us and know that there is no danger for them in this pond of ours way up here in the Green Forest. He is making sure, doubly sure. He led that flock of his all the way to the Sunny South last fall and now has led them all the long way back. No wonder he is called Old Faithful by those who follow him," said Paddy.

From the end of the pond where the Black Shadows were gathering rapidly came the sound of many light splashes and then the happy gabbling of many tongues increased. A few minutes later Honker himself swam over to the house in the water where Paddy and Mrs. Paddy waited.

"Welcome, old friend! It is good to have you back," cried Paddy.

"It is good to be back. Yes, sir, it is good to be back," declared the handsome great bird. He meant it. There was no doubt about that. And the members of his flock were just as glad.

As a rule there was no more quiet place in all the Green Forest than that small pond. Paddy and Mrs. Paddy are quiet folk and there are few sounds there but the occasional crash of a falling tree that they have cut, or once in a while the startling report of a broad tail hitting the water. But this pleasant evening it was a noisy place with the constant gabbling of many tongues. Those Geese had been flying since daybreak and were almost too tired to lift a wing. But it was their wings, not their tongues, that were tired. Have you noticed that some tongues seem never to tire?

All that long journey of many days Honker had led the way. High above rivers and ponds and great lakes, above vast forests, over farms and villages, and cities, they had flown steadily northward. Never for an instant had Honker hesitated in selecting the way they should go, and never for an instant had his followers questioned his leadership. In that flock were ambitious young ganders eager to be flock leaders some day, but not one so much as thought of questioning the judgment of wise old

Honker. That at all times he knew just where they were, and just where they were going, none ever doubted.

So it was that Honker had brought the flock safely to the little pond of his old friends in the Green Forest at the foot of the Great Mountain for the rest his tired followers so greatly needed. The flight that day had been the longest they had made on any day since leaving the Sunny South for their still far-away northern summer home. To some of the weary travelers it seemed that they couldn't possibly have managed another beat of their great wings.

To one of that tired flock reaching the little pond meant more than to any of the others. It was Mrs. Honker. Time after time that afternoon, especially in the latter part, she had thought she must drop out; that she hadn't the strength to keep on, but must go down on the next water they would pass over, go down and rest. Unable to keep up she would drop back.

Then would come an encouraging call from Honker, the faithful mate with whom she had made this long journey so many times before, a call meant just for her. He would slow the flight down a little and she would catch up.

It was the first time she ever had been a laggard. Always before she had held her place all day long up front next to Honker. This day she had been obliged to drop back and back until late in the afternoon she was the last one. Never had such a thing happened before.

No sooner were they on the water than Honker was at her

side, caressing her, talking to her in low tones. Could you have been there to see and hear, and could you have understood Goose talk, you would have seen and heard such loving tenderness as only those who are true mates for as long as both shall live can know. It is this way with the Geese and with their big snowy cousins, the Swans. It is so with King Eagle and a few others. Their love is for a lifetime. When it is given it is for always as long as the pair shall live. There is no divorce.

In the fall, on their way to the Sunny South, Mrs. Honker had been shot. One wing had been badly hurt. In time it had healed, but as yet had not regained full strength. This was why she had had such hard work keeping up with the flock this day, and at the last had lagged. Honker told Paddy all about it.

> Judge not the seeming laggard lest
> You find his pluck leads all the rest.

How this can be Mrs. Honker had shown that day.

"I hope she will feel rested in the morning," said Paddy.

"I hope so, too, for we still have far to go," Honker replied.

"I'll be all right; I'm sure I will. All I need is a good night's rest," said Mrs. Honker, who had joined them. She touched Honker's bill with her own.

Soon the gabbling of many tongues ceased. The dusky curtain of the night was drawn over the little pond in the Green Forest where with heads tucked under weary wings the tired travelers floated on the still water, perhaps dreaming of the still far-away homeland they were so eager to reach.

XVII. The Flock Goes

You often find where love abides
The heart and not the head decides.
                    —OLD MOTHER NATURE

IT WAS BREAK OF DAY and the Black Shadows were
hurrying away. Honker and his flock were awake and moving
restlessly at the first sign of the coming day. They had spent a
quiet, peaceful night. No hungry visitors had been around. Not
even Hooty the Owl had been over to the pond. Now the big
feathered travelers were eager to be on their way for another
long day of steady flying. It was the insistent call of the distant
homeland, the nesting grounds in the Far North.

Especially were the younger members of the flock impatient.

They had rested well. They had fully recovered from the weariness that had made that small pond such a welcome sight at the end of the long flight the day before. In the fall they had made the long journey south. Now they were making their first return flight. It was exciting. They were full of the spirit of adventure, and impatient of delay. Why didn't old Honker give the signal to start? Could he be going to stay over here for a day and another night? What was he waiting for? But none allowed impatience to question Honker. That wasn't to be thought of. It simply wasn't done.

At last came the signal. Honker's great wings lifted him into the air. Mrs. Honker followed. Then in order the others took their places in the flying wedge that Paddy and Mrs. Paddy watched slant upward over the tops of the trees to disappear straight toward the Far North. For a few minutes after the visitors had disappeared their voices floated back, becoming fainter and fainter until at last they were no longer heard.

"It was nice having them here. I wonder if we will see them again next spring," said Paddy. "Hello! Now who is coming?" he exclaimed a little later.

Low over the treetops came a lone Goose. It was Mrs. Honker. The two Beavers almost doubted their eyes. She came down on the water with a gentle splash, turned and swam over to them. In her eyes was a look of distress.

"What brings you back?" cried Paddy.

"I couldn't keep up," replied Mrs. Honker sadly.

"Is it because of that hurt wing?" Mrs. Paddy wanted to know.

Mrs. Honker nodded. "It just isn't strong enough," said she. "I guess the long flight yesterday was too much for it. Almost as soon as we left here this morning I knew I wouldn't be able to make another long flight again today. So I dropped out of the flock and came back. It seemed the only thing to do. I hope you don't mind."

"Of course we don't mind!" cried Paddy and Mrs. Paddy together.

"We'll be glad to have you stay as long as you want to," declared Mrs. Paddy. Paddy nodded approval.

"Does Honker know you have come back?" Mrs. Paddy wanted to know.

"I don't know," admitted Mrs. Honker. "I just kept dropping back because I couldn't keep up. At last I turned back and here I am. The flock must be a long way from here by this time." She said this mournfully.

"Listen!" cried Paddy.

"Honk, k'honk, onk, onk, k'honk."

There was no mistaking those voices. They grew louder and louder and louder still. In a few minutes the flock came in over the treetops and splashed down on the pond. At once Honker was beside Mrs. Honker, caressing her, talking to her in low gentle tones, anxiously asking questions. The others gathered around them all talking at once. Such gabbling! Such excitement! Mrs. Honker's return had upset the whole flock. There was no doubt of that.

"I wonder what they will do now," said Paddy.

"I wonder. Do you suppose that all will stay here?" said Mrs. Paddy.

For some time there was much noisy gabbling, all talking at once, and all excited. Anyway it seemed so to Paddy and Mrs. Paddy listening from the roof of their house. The rest of the flock crowded around Honker and Mrs. Honker, each trying to be heard above the others. Never had that usually quiet part of the Green Forest known such a noise. It brought other visitors to find out what was going on.

Lightfoot the Deer came silently down one of his little paths to the water's edge. He pretended that he had come for a drink. Buster Bear hurried there. In his eyes was a greedy look as he peered from back of a fallen tree. A Goose would be good eating at any time but extra good now when there was so little food. Now that he was fully awake from his long winter sleep he was getting very hungry, for he had had little to eat but a few roots he had dug up in damp places where the ground was no longer hard.

Tufty the Lynx, slipping soundlessly from cover to cover, sneaked unseen behind an old log at the water's edge. That noisy gabbling carried far through the Green Forest and caused Old Man Coyote to change his mind. On swift feet he made straight for the pond instead of hunting along the foot of the

Great Mountain as he had planned to do. Croaker the Raven came to find out what all the excitement was about.

It was still early in the morning. Even yet some of the Black Shadows were lingering. Each of that gabbling flock had an opinion of his or her own as to what should be done, and was expressing it.

"We came back just as soon as you were missed. Are you quite sure you can't go on today, my dear?" said Honker.

"Quite sure," replied Mrs. Honker. "Yesterday I strained that weak wing and this morning when we started I had hard work to keep up even a little way. As for flying all day, I just couldn't. So I came back. There was nothing else to do."

"Perhaps if we rest here for a few days that wing will get stronger. I'm sure rest is all it needs," ventured Honker.

At this there was a noisy outbreak of many tongues. Plainly the flock was badly upset. Some were for staying over, insisting that this was the right thing to do. Others protested that this would make them late in reaching the nesting grounds, the homeland in the Far North. Others were for slower, shorter flights to make it easier for Mrs. Honker to keep up. To this she shook her head.

"I can't go on yet, and I don't know when I will be able to," said she. "I'll stay here and rest. Perhaps later another flock will come along and I can join it. I will have to stay here a while. That is all there is to it."

"It is too bad Honker is the leader," said Paddy.

"Why?" asked Mrs. Paddy. She was puzzled. She couldn't see what that had to do with the matter and said so.

"Because he is her mate and if he were not the leader of the flock he could and probably would stay here with her. Being the leader he probably feels that he must go on with the flock. He has made the flight so often he knows all the safe feeding and resting places, and all the danger places and how to avoid them. The others know this and depend on him to lead them the best way," explained Paddy.

Some of the older ones who had followed Honker on the long flights for many seasons were for staying if he would not go with them, but some of the younger ones, who never had made the flight before, were eager, impatient and unafraid. They were for choosing a new leader and going on at once.

Honker and Mrs. Honker moved off a little to one side. They took no part in the noisy gabbling, but talked together in low tones. Suddenly Honker gave a loud honk. The noisy tongues instantly became still. The great birds sat on the water with their long necks stretched to full height, their eyes fixed on their leader. For a moment he faced them. Then he turned, gave the take-off signal, and his great wings lifted him in the air. He was headed straight north. The others followed in their usual order, all but Mrs. Honker. She remained on the water. She honked once as she watched them disappear over the treetops. It was a forlorn, lonesome sound.

XVIII. A Lonely Lady

No loneliness is half so great
As love deserted by a mate.
— OLD MOTHER NATURE

IT IS TOO BAD. It certainly is," said Paddy. He was watching Mrs. Honker. She was swimming about aimlessly. Now and then she would stop and float, her long neck held high, staring to the north where Honker, the mate from whom she never had been parted before through all the years since they first met long ago, had gone.

"It is a shame. That is what it is, a shame," declared Mrs. Paddy. There was no doubt whatever that she meant it.

"What is a shame?" asked Paddy.

"For Honker to leave her alone this way. I didn't think it of him. No, sir, I didn't think he would do such a thing," replied Mrs. Paddy.

Mrs. Honker swam over near them. "He *had* to go," she said in a low voice as if she had overheard Mrs. Paddy. She hadn't. She was talking to herself. It is doubtful if she was aware of her neighbors. "He *had* to go," she repeated.

"Why did he have to go? Why couldn't he have stayed with you?" Mrs. Paddy asked.

"He is the leader of the flock," replied Mrs. Honker. She said it proudly, as if it explained everything, as in fact it did.

"Couldn't someone else lead the flock?" asked Paddy.

"Not as he does. The others wouldn't trust a new leader as they do Honker. They know he knows. He does too. He knows every feeding place, every danger place. He knows when to fly high and when to fly low. He knows when to stop and when to go on. He knows when there will be a change in the weather, when the waters ahead will be free of ice, everything that should be known for the good of all. Only one who can be wholly trusted can be a true leader. Honker is a true leader. So of course he had to go." Mrs. Honker said this simply, as if there could be no question that it was the right thing to do.

Mrs. Paddy waited until Mrs. Honker was where she couldn't hear. Then she spoke her mind. "He deserted her," she declared. "He's selfish. He thinks more of being a leader than he does of her. Would you do such a thing to me? Would you leave me like that?"

Paddy grinned. "How should I know? I haven't any wings. There is no knowing what I might do if I had wings," he teased.

She paid no attention. "Right now Mrs. Honker is terribly lonely, poor thing, and she is going to be more so," said Mrs. Paddy. "We'll be nice to her and try to make her feel at home. But that won't be enough to make her happy. Honker belongs *here*. Probably he has forgotten her already." Mrs. Paddy was indignant. There was no doubt of that.

Mrs. Honker paddled about aimlessly. She kept listening for the honking and gabbling of familiar voices though she knew she wouldn't hear them. She had no appetite, which was just as well for there was little in that pond that a Goose could eat. A lonely lady was Mrs. Honker, and growing more so. All the long day she paddled about without purpose, or sat for long periods staring into the north. Just before the coming of the Black Shadows, she climbed up on the roof of the house in the water.

"She shows good sense," remarked Paddy.

"Of course she does. She is a sensible person. Just what is she showing good sense about now?" replied Mrs. Paddy.

"Getting up on the roof of our house to spend the night. It is the safest place she can be. Nobody but Hooty the Owl can get to her there, and he isn't likely to see her if she doesn't move. She won't look like anything alive, and Hooty won't give her a second look," replied Paddy.

"Listen!" interrupted Mrs. Paddy.

Both listened. There was no mistaking that sound for there is no other like it. "*Honk, k'honk, onk, onk, k'honk.*" Could it be that they were to have more visitors, another flock on the way to the nesting homeland? But this was not the gabbling of many tongues, just a lone voice, and it was coming from the *wrong* direction, the north!

They looked over at Mrs. Honker. She was standing now, her head held high, her wings half lifted. Her eyes were fixed on the darkening sky to the north. Suddenly she honked. It was a sound of pure joy. Because it was pure joy it held a sweetness hard to believe possible in the voice of a Goose. Back came an answer no less joyous. Mrs. Honker was honking now as if she couldn't stop even for breath.

Then against the sky they saw him coming, a single great bird on swift wings, his long neck stretched full length, his great wings driving him faster as he neared the pond. Now they were set for a long glide to the water. Mrs. Honker had slipped from the roof and was half swimming, half flying to meet him.

"It is Honker! He has come back!" cried Mrs. Paddy.

Such gentle caressing of each other as followed! Such soft, tender, loving talk! It wasn't necessary to understand the words to get the meaning. Not since it was first made had that little pond deep in the Green Forest seen such pure happiness.

Paddy's curiosity tipped his tongue with questions. "Where are the others, the flock?" he wanted to know.

"Probably they have settled somewhere for the night," replied Honker.

"Are they going to wait for you?" was the next question.

Honker shook his head. "They have another leader now. He has made the trip with us before. He'll find the way. I made sure he was started right, then came back. When I left here this morning I left my heart behind me," said he.

Mrs. Honker moved a little closer to him. She reached over and stroked his neck with her bill.

That quiet little pond was a lovely place in which to rest. It would have been quite perfect had there been food. There wasn't; not their kind of food. But it was not too far to a place where there was food. Perhaps it was well that they had to make these daily trips, for this regular use of Mrs. Honker's weak wing strengthened it. So the days passed.

"Do you think they will nest here?" Mrs. Paddy asked.

"I wish they would. It would be nice to have them for neighbors all summer," replied Paddy.

"Do you really think so?" asked Mrs. Paddy.

Paddy looked up quickly. "Don't you?" he asked.

"Yes and no," said Mrs. Paddy. "They are good neighbors. We couldn't have better. I love to see them. They are a handsome pair. But they draw a lot of attention. Haven't you noticed?"

"What of it?" asked Paddy.

"It is the wrong kind of attention. I mean it is from the wrong folks," replied Mrs. Paddy. "Since they arrived there has been hardly a time day or night when someone hasn't been prowling around this pond hoping for a dinner of Goose, and just as ready for a Beaver dinner. If the Honkers should nest and try to raise a family this pond would be altogether too popular for my peace of mind, or yours. Don't tell them I said so, but I hope they won't think of nesting here. You know we will have our own children to think of."

They were sitting on the dam. Paddy was carefully combing his fur with the special split combing claws of which he has one on each hind foot. He looked thoughtful. "My dear," said he, "I believe you are right. It hadn't occurred to me before. It is just as you say. Probably at least one pair of hungry eyes is watching this pond this very minute."

At that very time in another part of the pond Honker and Mrs. Honker were trying to decide what to do. "I guess we will have to nest here," said Honker.

Mrs. Honker looked longingly to the north. She sighed. Honker heard the sigh and understood what it meant, and just how she felt. "Perhaps we can find a better place to nest without going all the way," he suggested. "We must decide something soon for it will soon be too late for nesting," he added.

That evening a small belated flock from the Sunny South spent the night in the pond. At daybreak the big eager birds were on their way. With them went Honker and Mrs. Honker.

"I'm sorry they have gone and I'm glad," said Mrs. Paddy.
Paddy understood. He felt the same way.

XIX. Buster Bear's Great Fright

Those who grumble and complain
Very little ever gain.
— OLD MOTHER NATURE

BUSTER BEAR was grumbling and complaining. Usually those who grumble and complain the most are the ones who have little or nothing to do. They seem to find a queer sort of pleasure in grumbling and complaining. Buster Bear is one of these. Now as he grumbled and complained it wasn't to anybody, for there was nobody around to listen to him. Perhaps it was because he had nothing else to do, or because he liked to hear the sound of his own voice.

"It is too hot," grumbled Buster. "It has been too hot too long. I've never known such a hot summer. It is too dry, much too dry. Berries are no good because they are dried up. Everything is dried up, or will be if there isn't rain soon. I never was so uncomfortable in my life. I think I'll go over to Paddy's pond and try to cool off. No, I won't. It is too far. Probably the water is too warm anyway. It was the last time I was there. Didn't feel any cooler after a bath, only wet. Was hotter than ever afterward. Phew, what a day!"

He shuffled about aimlessly. It was too hot to be moving about and it was too hot to lie still. He thought again of Paddy's pond and wished he were there. He turned that way, then changed his mind again, although it really was only a little way. He came to a big, partly rotted old stump in a small clearing. Usually he delighted in digging his claws into such an old stump and pulling it apart to look for grubs or possibly Mice. Now he reached out a big black paw. Then he drew it back and sat down panting.

"Probably nothing in there," he grumbled. "Anyway it is too much work and too hot to find out. I haven't any appetite. When it is too hot for me to eat it is hot. Yes, sir, it is hot."

Looking up he saw, showing above the tops of the trees, great masses of clouds towering up like mountains in the sky. They were what are called thunderheads. Buster knew what they meant. He had often seen such clouds before. For the first time he noticed the stillness all about. Not a leaf stirred. It was as if old Mother Nature was expecting something to happen and was holding her breath while she waited. Buster Bear began to feel uneasy. He grew more and more uneasy as he watched the clouds rise higher and higher until they hid the face of bright, hot Mr. Sun. The day became dark. Thunder rumbled and lightning streaked across the sky.

"There will be rain at last, but it will be the kind of storm I don't like. I better find a place where I will be out of it, and find it in a hurry," grumbled Buster. He began to run and as he ran he became more uneasy than ever. Something surely was going to happen. He always had that feeling before a thunderstorm. The truth is great big Buster Bear was scared.

He remembered that not far away was a big windfall. In some great windstorm a number of trees had been uprooted and blown over so that they had fallen in a great tangled pile. He could creep under that windfall and be out of the wind which now was beginning to blow and would soon blow harder. And under there he could keep fairly dry no matter how hard the rain fell. He knew all about that windfall. He had slept under it often.

The storm was coming fast now. The lightning flashed with little time between the flashes. To Buster it seemed as if his heart jumped with every flash. He was sure it did with every terrific clap of thunder. Now he could see the tall pine tree at the very edge of the big windfall. It was the tallest tree anywhere around. At the foot of it was the opening under the windfall. He was almost there when the first drops of rain fell.

He never did get there. Came a blinding flash of lightning

and with it a crash of thunder that shook the ground under his feet. He fell heels over head, scrambled to his feet and just as part of the tall pine came crashing to the ground he plunged away from there. He ran blindly, not seeing where he was going. He bumped into trees and tumbled over logs. He was bawling with fright. Yes, sir, Buster Bear was bawling with fright. He didn't know what had happened. But you know. Lightning had struck and shattered that tall tree.

Often folks are lucky and don't know it. So it was now with Buster Bear. He really was a very lucky Bear, very lucky indeed. But he didn't know it. He was sure he was the unluckiest Bear in all the Great World. He stepped in a hole he didn't see and fell headlong. He picked himself up and plunged on, not seeing where he was going and not caring so long as he got away. He tripped over a stick and fell again. Never before in his whole life had he had such a terrible fright. I guess you would have been just as frightened as he was. I am sure I would. No wonder he was sure he was the unluckiest Bear in all the Great World.

Yet all the time he was perhaps the luckiest Bear in all the Great World. Had he been a moment sooner in starting for that windfall he would have been right at the very foot of that tall pine when the lightning struck it. Coming down the tree to the ground it almost certainly would have hit and killed Buster. In a thunderstorm there is a no more dangerous place to be than under a tree. The bigger and taller the tree the more likely it is to be hit by lightning, and so the greater the danger. The Green

Forest folk haven't yet learned this. That is why Buster didn't know that he really was lucky instead of unlucky.

Looking back over his shoulder he saw something that added to his fright if that were possible. It was the thing that the Green Forest and Green Meadow folk, big and little, fear more than anything else or anyone. It was the Red Terror. That is what they call fire. It is a good name, for fire is truly a terrible thing, a very terrible thing, when it is out of control. It eats up everything in its way, the trees, the bushes, the grass, the leaves and sticks on the ground, everything but the earth itself. Before it the biggest of the Green Forest folks, like Flathorns the Moose and Buster Bear, are helpless unless they can get to water, as helpless as the smallest folks. Their only chance to live is to get enough of a start to run or fly to a place of safety before it can catch them. It can and sometimes does race through the Green Forest faster than those with the swiftest feet can run. Fire is Man's willing servant, but when it gets away from him it becomes the Red Terror and often is his master, a dreadful one.

As Buster looked back the Red Terror was just starting, but it was starting fast. It was in the fallen top of the tall pine tree. Even as Buster looked it began running through the big windfall. It ran fast because the long drought had made everything so very, very dry. It snapped and crackled and roared. The drier things are the faster they are eaten up by the Red Terror, and the faster it can rush on its terrible way.

Buster had seen the Red Terror before. He knew what it

could do and would do if nothing stopped it. It would leave the whole Great Mountain black and lifeless excepting in the pond of the Beaver folks, and such other ponds as there were. No Green Forest would be left. The wind was blowing hard and this was bad, for it helped to spread the Red Terror, driving it on faster and faster. All the time lightning was flashing and thunder crashing.

It was the lightning that had started the Red Terror when it struck the tall pine, for lightning is a kind of fire. Forest fires often are started in just this way, although all too often they are started by the carelessness of Man. Now the Red Terror was running up trees and jumping across from top to top, at the same time racing fast in the leaves on the ground. It was rushing straight after Buster. Already he felt the hot breath of it. The smoke blown ahead of it choked him. It was hard to breathe. If only he could reach the pond of Paddy the Beaver and plunge in before the Red Terror should catch him! But could he?

Rain was falling but it seemed not to check the Red Terror. It seemed to Buster that he couldn't run another step. He was gasping for air. Through the trees he could see the pond just a little way ahead. But the Red Terror was almost at his heels. He was in despair.

Right then it seemed to Buster as if a whole pond had been dropped all at once from the sky. Never had he seen so much water fall all at once. It was what is called a cloudburst. All the water in a cloud seems to be dropped at one time. It makes sudden floods. It did now, threatening to wash out Paddy's dam. But it didn't last long. The dam was still there. But there was no Red Terror. It had been drowned. The very storm that had started the Red Terror had ended it. Such things do happen.

Yes, Buster Bear was a lucky Bear, but he didn't know it.

XX. A Rumor Proves True

A little fun, a little play,
Should be a part of every day.
— LITTLE JOE OTTER

A LAZY SUMMER, a busy autumn, had passed and it was once more early winter in the Beaver pond in the Green Forest at the foot of the Great Mountain.

"My dear," said Paddy to Mrs. Paddy, "I still think that we are the only people in the Green Forest who really know how to live. I do for a fact."

They were in the comfortable big living room which was also their bedroom in the big house in the water. It was dark in there, for there were no windows and the doorway was in the floor. They liked the darkness. Like many other Green Forest

133

folk they have eyes adapted to darkness. They would have been most uncomfortable and unhappy had bright sunlight been pouring into their house.

Mrs. Paddy stopped chewing a piece of bark to say that she had known that for as long as she could remember. "I really don't understand how some folks I might mention manage to live through winter," she concluded.

"Nor do I," replied Paddy. He turned a stick to get at the bark on the other side. "Certainly none of our neighbors live more comfortably than we do, and I can't think of any who live as comfortably. Here we are in a warm, dry house, with plenty to eat and nothing to worry about, not a thing."

"Not even the weather," said Mrs. Paddy.

"Not even the weather," agreed Paddy. "Not many can say that. Snow, sleet, rain, sunshine, it is all the same to us. So far as we are concerned rough Brother North Wind might just as well hold his breath. Half the time we don't even know he is around. Jack Frost cannot bother us. We never go hungry because we can get what we need from our food pile under the ice and do it without danger, exposure or discomfort of any kind. We eat when we're hungry and sleep when we're sleepy, swim under the ice for exercise when we feel like it. And all without anything at all to worry about."

"Excepting one thing," said Mrs. Paddy. She began chewing another piece of bark.

"And what is that, if you please?" demanded Paddy.

"The dam. You know as well as I do what a leak in that could lead to. You haven't forgotten what happened last winter? Anyway, I haven't," replied Mrs. Paddy mildly.

"That isn't a cause for worry any more, and never will be as long as we look it over every day and stop small leaks. Last winter the dam was new. It is bigger and stronger now, and it doesn't worry me one bit. Speaking of the dam reminds me that I haven't been over to it today. I'll swim over there now and take this bare stick with me just in case there should be some use for it," said Paddy.

Taking the stick with him he disappeared through the doorway in the floor. Mrs. Paddy kept on eating. When she had eaten the last bit of bark on that stick she took it outside intending to take it over to the dam. Then she changed her mind. She was feeling drowsy as most folks so often feel after a hearty meal. She left the bare stick outside and returned to the big room for a nap on her comfortable bed of shredded wood. She awoke when Paddy returned.

"Was there a leak in the dam you had to fix? You've been gone a long time," said she sleepily.

"There wasn't any leak. The dam is all right. I went over to that little open place where Laughing Brook brings the water into our pond. I put my head out there for a look around and on the chance that I might pick up a bit of news," explained Paddy.

"Did you pick up any news?" asked Mrs. Paddy without interest. She was still sleepy.

135

"I heard a rumor," replied Paddy.

"What was it?" Mrs. Paddy wanted to know.

"I heard that Little Joe Otter has been seen around the mouth of Laughing Brook where it joins the Big River," said Paddy.

"What of it? That is a long, long way from here, so why worry?" replied Mrs. Paddy. She yawned.

"I'm not worrying," retorted Paddy indignantly. "Just the same I hope he'll stay there and not take it into his head to come up Laughing Brook. I would rather he should be there than here."

He wasn't really worrying, but the rumor did make him uneasy. Little Joe Otter is a great traveler even in winter. He doesn't care how cold the weather may be. He doesn't mind snow and he doesn't mind ice. If fishing isn't good in one place he moves on to another place. He is a famous fisherman, you know. For a long way up and down the Big River he knows all the brooks flowing into it, and these he knows all the way up to where they begin. He knows all the pools and all the rapids. He knows all the holes in and along the banks, and all the secret places wherein to rest in peace and comfort. He knows the best banks for sliding in both summer and winter. He knows the kinds of fish in each brook and which are the best eating. He knows the best places to cross on land from brook to brook and often uses them, especially in winter. He is just as much at home on one brook as on another. So Paddy knew that if Little Joe took it into his head to come up Laughing Brook to the foot of the Great Mountain the distance wouldn't bother him at all.

"That fellow is the only one who can make any trouble for us at this time of year," said Paddy. "He is the only one who can follow us under the ice. Anywhere we can go he can go, so I would just as soon not have him around."

"Are you afraid of him?" asked Mrs. Paddy softly.

"No," replied Paddy shortly. "You know I'm not afraid of him. Nor is he afraid of me. We just don't like each other. When folks don't like each other little things can make a lot of trouble, and a fight often springs from nothing. So it is better that we should not be neighbors. I don't want to fight, so I hope he will stay away from here. I don't want him around."

So while Paddy wasn't really afraid he was uneasy. He couldn't help being so. Every day he visited the open water at the head of the pond, hoping that he might see someone who had seen Little Joe Otter and so knew where he was and what he was doing. Then, too, he knew that should Little Joe come up there to the pond it was at that opening he would enter the pond, for it was the only place he could get under the ice.

"If he should come he isn't likely to stay. There is nothing here to interest him, nothing to keep him here," said Mrs. Paddy.

"I wish I could think so," said Paddy.

"I guess you can if you really try. What makes you think you can't?" asked Mrs. Paddy.

"The fish, my dear. It is because of the fish," replied Paddy.

"The fish? What fish? And what have fish got to do with it?" demanded Mrs. Paddy wonderingly.

"My dear, don't tell me that you haven't noticed what a lot of Trout are in our pond, more than ever before!" exclaimed Paddy.

"Now you mention it I have noticed it," admitted Mrs. Paddy. "But I haven't given the matter a thought. I am so used to seeing them about when I am swimming that I haven't paid any attention to them. If we were eaters of fish probably I would have taken more notice of them. But what have those fish to do with Little Joe Otter and his staying here if he comes?"

"Little Joe Otter eats fish. At times he lives on them. He is especially fond of Trout. So I will be best pleased if he doesn't pay us a visit," explained Paddy.

Days passed and Paddy heard no more rumors. He had about decided that the rumor he had heard was nothing but a rumor and not founded on fact. Then one day when he visited the open water he swam a little way up Laughing Brook where the water ran too swiftly to freeze over excepting in the very coldest weather. At one place a little beyond him the bank on one side was high and steep. He looked over to it just in time to see a brown form glide down it and disappear in the water.

"Little Joe Otter!" exclaimed Paddy under his breath.

Hastily he swam to a place where he could watch that bank with little likelihood of being seen. He saw Little Joe, who was little in name only, come out of the water at a place where the bank was low, run up to where the bank was highest and steepest, then flat on his stomach with legs held straight behind him, his front legs at his sides, slide down headfirst. Swoosh! he went into the black water. Little Joe Otter was sliding for fun. He couldn't be doing it for anything else. He was having a good time and he showed it.

So the rumor Paddy had heard had proved true.

XXI. Neighbors But Not Neighborly

*In some things folks may disagree
But still the best of neighbors be.*

—OLD MOTHER NATURE

LITTLE JOE OTTER was having fun. There was no doubt about that. He had made a slippery slide down a steep bank where the water was not frozen over. Over and over again he slid down this, flat on his stomach, swoosh into the water.

It was a mild day, just right for sliding, and he was making the most of it. After a while he grew tired of sliding. "Enough is enough," said he. "That must be the pond of Paddy the Beaver that this brook is running into. I wonder if Paddy and

Mrs. Paddy are living there this winter. I'll swim over and find out."

He found out sooner than he expected. Paddy, unseen, had been watching him slide and now showed himself. "So you are still living here," said Little Joe.

"I am still living here," replied Paddy, not too pleasantly.

"And Mrs. Paddy?" inquired his unwelcome visitor.

"She is still living here too," replied Paddy.

Little Joe shook his round head. "I don't see how you do it," said he.

"Do what?" asked Paddy.

"Stay so long in one place. I wouldn't if I could, and I couldn't if I would, which I guess is just as well," replied Little Joe.

"Why can't you?" asked Paddy.

"Food," replied Little Joe. "There never are enough fish and clams for us Otters to stay very long in one place. So we have to keep on the move and go where the food is. But that is half the fun of being alive. What do you folks who stay in one place know about the Great World? Nothing. Simply nothing. I don't see how you stand it."

"We know when we are well off, and how to stay so. That is more than some folks seem to know," growled Paddy. He wasn't polite. He wasn't feeling polite.

"Speaking of fish reminds me that I would like a fat Trout right now. There must be some in this pond," declared the sleek brown fisherman.

"It is my pond," Paddy said sharply.

"You don't say," grinned Little Joe Otter. "Well, the fish in it are my fish, or will be when I catch them. You keep the pond and I'll take the fish. What do you say?" He grinned again.

Paddy didn't say. He didn't know what to say. "You know you can't keep me out of that pond if you try," said Little Joe good-naturedly.

"I haven't said anything about trying to keep you out of my pond," grumbled Paddy.

"Don't," said Little Joe. "Just remember that I go where I please, when I please, and do what I please. I'm not quarrelsome, but I'm not afraid to fight anybody who interferes with me."

"Are you planning to stay long?" ventured Paddy.

Again Little Joe grinned. "That depends on how long the fish last. If there are plenty of Trout in your pond I'll be around for a while anyway. Any objections?" said he.

Paddy offered no objections. "As long as you eat fish and we don't, and we eat bark and you don't, I guess Mrs. Paddy and I will find nothing to fight with you about. The fish are all yours for the catching," said he.

"And the bark is all yours. Imagine eating bark! Ugh!" Little Joe made up a face. Then he dived under the ice for a fish and Paddy dived under the ice to go home and tell Mrs. Paddy the news.

So Little Joe Otter became a neighbor to Paddy and Mrs. Paddy, but they were not neighborly. Little Joe paid no atten-

142

tion to the others even though this was their pond. In truth he was a little scornful of them.

"Those folks don't know how to live. They do nothing but eat and sleep. They don't have any fun at all," thought he scornfully.

"That fellow does nothing but fish and play," said Paddy with equal scorn.

Under water in the bank on which Little Joe had made his slippery slide was a hole leading up to a warm dry chamber. Little Joe didn't know who had dug it and didn't care. He had possession of it now and it would suit him perfectly for as long as he chose to stay. So he continued to be a neighbor, but without neighborliness. It often is that way with the Green Forest folk. They live near together yet have nothing to do with each other. They simply live and let live.

Little Joe is sharp. He has to be. He has something for which he is envied by mankind — his beautiful, warm fur coat. So excepting in summer he must be constantly on guard to save that precious coat and with it his more precious life.

He was returning from a trip far up the brook. In the distance he heard a harsh voice and stopped to listen. He knew that voice. There was no mistaking it. It was the voice of Croaker the Raven.

"Old Croaker sees someone he doesn't like. I can tell by the way he croaks," thought Little Joe. He listened a moment longer with growing suspicion and distrust.

He hurried on, but hurrying didn't prevent him having a little fun. What boy or girl seeing smooth ice ahead can resist the temptation to run a few steps, then slide? It makes fun of an errand or even of going to school. Little Joe travels in much the same way when he can. With short bounds he gets up speed, then throws himself forward flat on his stomach, sliding as far as he can on ice or through snow. There he makes a long furrow each time.

When he came to the open water where he had made his slippery slide he moved slowly, carefully, using eyes and nose constantly. He saw nothing and smelled nothing to make him suspect anything might be wrong. He was just being careful. He no longer heard Croaker the Raven. He wished Croaker would come his way so that he might ask whom Croaker had seen. But Croaker didn't, and Little Joe was extra careful for whoever Croaker had seen might have come this way.

He circled around to the top of the slippery slide. Everything seemed as always but he had a feeling of uneasiness. He looked down the slippery slide but he didn't go down. That uneasy feeling might be a warning. He had known dreadful things to happen to Otters down under water at the bottom of slippery slides. He circled around and entered the water at a place he never had used before. He swam back and forth watching both banks, but saw nothing wrong. Finally he swam to the low place where he had been in the habit of climbing out.

He didn't climb out there now. He felt as if someone had

whispered not to; that there was danger there. Of course no one had. It was just that uneasy feeling. He swam to where the water was frozen over, climbed out on the ice and went ashore. There he found signs that someone had been there recently. Carefully he smelled all about. At last he got just the faintest of scents, but faint as it was he knew it instantly. It was the hated Man smell. One of those two-legged folks distrusted by all who live in the Green Forest had been there. That was whom old Croaker had seen. He knew now all he needed to know. He slid into the water and headed for Paddy's pond. He suddenly felt hungry.

He caught a Trout and climbed out on the ice to eat it just as Paddy appeared. He looked over at Paddy and said, "I'll miss these good trout."

Paddy pricked up his ears as much as such short round ears can be pricked up. "What do you mean you'll miss them?" he asked.

"Unless I find more just as good," said Little Joe as if finishing his statement.

Paddy's ears were open their widest. "Have you caught all the Trout in my pond?" he asked.

"No," said Little Joe, shaking his head.

"Are you going away?" asked Paddy bluntly.

"I'm thinking of it," admitted Little Joe.

"Why? Don't you like it here any more?" Paddy wanted to know.

145

"I'll feel safer somewhere else," said Little Joe.

Paddy looked surprised. He was surprised. "I thought you were not afraid of anybody. There is no danger here," said he.

"Perhaps not for you, but I'll feel safer somewhere else," replied Little Joe. Then he told Paddy of the Man smell. "When I find that along a brook I know it is time for me to move on. It has been nice seeing you. I'll see you again sometime," he concluded. He turned and went bounding and sliding off through the woods.

"Hi! Where are you going?" cried Paddy. Little Joe didn't answer. He was taking the shortest way overland to another brook.

"I wonder if he is easily frightened or is really smart," thought Paddy. And that is just what a trapper wondered as he visited his empty traps, one of them set right where Little Joe had been in the habit of climbing the bank where it was low.

So once more there was peace and an end of worry, for the law allowed no trapping of Beavers. The joy of work well done, of simple homemaking, of quiet living, and the happiness of contentment left nothing wanting at the pond of Paddy the Beaver deep in the Green Forest at the foot of the Great Mountain.

THE END